Mrs. Searwood's Secret Weapon

Mrs. Searwood's Secret Weapon

LEONARD WIBBERLEY

Illustrations by Warren Chappell

COACHWHIP PUBLICATIONS

Greenville, Ohio

Mrs. Searwood's Secret Weapon, by Leonard Wibberley
© 2015 Coachwhip Publications

Published 1954, no renewal.
No claims made on public domain material.

Leonard Wibberley (1915-1983)

ISBN 1-61646-290-6
ISBN-13 978-1-61646-290-1

CoachwhipBooks.com

CONTENTS

TO MY MOTHER

Mrs. Sinaid Wibberley

WHO, REGARDING WARFARE AS AN
INTOLERABLE INTERFERENCE WITH
NORMAL LIVING, REFUSED TO LEAVE
HER FLAT IN LONDON DURING THE
RECENT HOSTILITIES

ALL THE CHARACTERS in this work are imaginary, with three exceptions. Since this is a historical fantasy it has been necessary to introduce at least one public figure in a role which, though it has no basis whatever in fact, is not, I trust, at odds with his character. I hope that Sir Winston Churchill will take no exception to this liberty. Of Chief White Feather and Old Grady I can only say that while it is impossible to prove their existence, that in itself is no proof that they do not exist.

The Author

CHAPTER ONE

MRS. SEARWOOD PICKED UP her handbag, smiled at the attendant in the ladies' lounge of Barker Brothers store in Kensington and walked out to the High Street, to wait for a Number Eleven bus which would take her to her flat in Westminster.

It was two o'clock of a Monday afternoon, and there were not many people about. Mrs. Searwood was glad of that. Getting onto crowded busses was more and more of a struggle these days, and lately she had found herself unfairly handicapped in the combat, in which previously she had taken some relish. This was because one of her garters had broken—a minor misfortune in better times but now, with the war five years old and rationing at its peak, a major disaster. It was impossible to get the ration coupons for another girdle. It was impossible to get elastic to repair the garter. And so she had had to twist her stocking in a knot at the top to hold it in place. The stocking usually held up all right until it came to struggling to get on a bus in a crowd of people, when it quite frequently fell down. This Mrs. Searwood found embarrassing in the extreme. She just couldn't understand why the Prime Minister didn't have the Minister of Supply in and tell him plainly that whatever the plight of King and Empire, it was not necessary for elderly ladies to walk garterless around London in order to achieve victory.

She turned now to peer down the road for a sight of her bus and saw with surprise that there was someone standing behind her, although there had been no one there a moment before. At first glance, she appreciated only that this someone was a very tall man. But as she turned away, wondering how he could have come up so quietly, she suddenly realized that he hadn't any clothes on.

"Good heavens," said Mrs. Searwood out loud and turned again. It was true. The man was over six feet tall, heavily sun-tanned, and except for what she vaguely realized was a breechcloth, was completely nude. She was so shocked that for a second she could say nothing and then retreated behind platitudes to recover from her confusion.

"It *is* rather warm for the time of the year, isn't it?" she ventured nervously.

The stranger nodded his head gravely, but made no further reply.

"You're a Commando, I suppose?" she said. Mrs. Searwood had heard that Commandos were given all sorts of strange assignments to test their endurance and resourcefulness and it crossed her mind that this might be one undergoing such a test.

"No," said the stranger.

"Bombed out, eh? My daughter Priscilla's husband was bombed out and had to go around in his pyjamas for three days. He lost all his clothes and caught a shocking cold."

"No, I wasn't bombed out," replied the stranger. He looked anxiously up and down the street as if to see if there was anyone in sight.

"Get into that doorway," he ordered brusquely.

Mrs. Searwood experienced a flush of dismay and suspected the worst.

"Young man," she said, "don't you dare lay a hand on me. I'll call the police. I'm an elderly woman and don't you touch me." She realized with horror that she hadn't brought her umbrella. It was the one weapon which she felt was reliable for repulsing the attacks of those men who (she had been warned from childhood) infested the streets of every city day and night, hoping to find a female alone.

"Don't argue," said the stranger fiercely. "Do as you're told!"

"I won't," said Mrs. Searwood.

"Hurry!" shouted the stranger and his voice, sharp and imperative, had a quality to it that made her retreat, against her will, into the doorway. As she did so she was conscious that underlying her own fears, she was worried about what Priscilla would think. Priscilla was always warning her about talking to strangers and she would not understand.

She had now backed into the doorway as far as she could go, her heavy bag gripped firmly in her right hand as her only weapon of defense. To her surprise, the stranger made no move towards her, but remained standing at the bus stop, looking up anxiously at the sky.

Suddenly there was the roar of an airplane flying low. The sound of the engines, trapped between the rows of houses and shops, reverberated back and forth with appalling effect. Noise piled upon noise, buffeted around in the deserted street until it seemed almost possible to see and touch the chaos and confusion. Mrs. Searwood peeked up and saw that there wasn't just one plane but two, the one in pursuit of the other, its machine guns crackling so that the leading edge of the wing seemed to be on fire. Bullets ripped the surface of the street and ricocheted off the pavement where she had been standing but a moment before. And then, as swiftly as they had come, the two planes were gone, leaving her dazed and trembling.

The stranger was still standing by the bus stop, miraculously unhurt.

"You can come out now," he said, rather smugly, "it's all over."

"And thank goodness too," said Mrs. Searwood. A wave of unreasoning anger at having been so frightened swept over her. "What do you mean by frightening me like that?" she demanded. "I thought you were going to . . . I thought you were . . . Well, you know perfectly well what I thought, standing there with practically nothing on and telling me to get into the doorway. I've a good mind to tell the police."

The stranger smiled.

"I only meant to protect you," he said. "I'm sorry if I frightened you while doing it." His voice sounded friendly and a little concerned.

"Who are you anyway?" Mrs. Searwood demanded.

"I'm an Indian."

"That's just what I said," Mrs. Searwood retorted. "You're an American Indian. One of those Rangers . . . and you said you weren't a Commando."

"No madam," replied the stranger, "I'm not a Ranger or a Commando. But I am an American Indian. It's too complicated to explain now and anyway, if people see you talking to me, they won't understand. You see, I'm what you call dead."

"You're *dead?*" said Mrs. Searwood. "Why, that's nonsense. I can see you standing there as large as life."

"You can," said the Indian. "But other people can't. I'm a spirit. An apparition. I've materialized to you but I'm invisible to everyone else. It is, as I said, a complicated thing to explain. But if you'll give me an opportunity—allow me, perhaps, to accompany you to your home, I can make everything quite clear."

Mrs. Searwood was about to reply, but the Number Eleven bus for which she had been waiting pulled up to the curb and the conductor called out, "Come on. Come on. Can't wait around here all day. I'm late already what with having to pull over to the side for them blinkin' airplanes. Must be a hot one to be chasing it so low." He leaned down to Mrs. Searwood and almost pulled her aboard.

The Indian leaped lightly on behind, walked through the conductor, and stood politely in the aisle waiting for her to be seated.

"Well," said Mrs. Searwood, "it's a relief at least to know that you are a gentleman."

"Thank you ma'am," said the conductor. "Thank you indeed."

CHAPTER TWO

THE JOURNEY TO WESTMINSTER took just over half an hour on the bus, and Mrs. Searwood could not recall a longer half hour in all her fifty-four years. The Indian sat on the seat beside her and this she found embarrassing. She wanted to question him further, but since he was invisible to others, decided against it. She studied him surreptitiously and decided reluctantly that he was perhaps the most handsome figure of a man she had ever seen in her life. He was magnificently muscled and his aquiline features looked all the sharper because of his head, which was clean shaven except for a top knot.

It surprised her that others could not see him, for there he was as solid as a house though she noted with a little quirk of awe that it was not necessary for him to breathe. There was no movement of the chest to indicate the drawing in or expelling of breath.

The bus conductor certainly couldn't see him, for he asked for but one fare, and passed by her seat twice without as much as a sidelong glance. At Hyde Park Corner, a man got on and for a terrible moment looked as though he was going to sit down on the Indian's lap. But he thought better of it and moved further up front. Mrs. Searwood decided then to put her bag down on the seat to discourage others from sitting there. But the Indian placed it on his lap so that it would appear to the rest of the passengers to be suspended several inches off the upholstery. Mrs. Searwood took it quickly back.

13

"Are you quite sure nobody can see you?" she whispered out of the side of her mouth as she had seen race-course tipsters do in the movies.

"Absolutely," replied the Indian. "You're the first one to see me in over three hundred years."

"Well, can't they hear you talking?"

"No. Oh, sometimes I can make them hear me if I want to. It amuses me occasionally. Would you like a demonstration?" Before Mrs. Searwood could stop him, he put his fingers in his mouth and emitted a high-pitched whistle.

Everyone turned to look at her, and the bus driver was so surprised that he swerved and nearly ran into a taxi. The conductor came up, his slow and deliberate walk the embodiment of official dignity. "Now then, mother," he said in gentle reproof, "none of your carryings-on. Ought to take a little more water with it. You know what they calls gin — mother's ruin." Mrs. Searwood opened her mouth to protest, but realized it was hopeless and tried to make herself inconspicuous by squeezing down in the seat.

"Don't you ever do that again," she whispered fiercely. "You behave just as if you were brought up in a wigwam."

"I was," the Indian replied. She glared at him and turned away to look out of the window and ignore him completely.

They got off by the Houses of Parliament and when the bus had gone Mrs. Searwood turned to the Indian and said, "I don't know that I like the idea of you coming to my flat. You've got me very confused. I'm not at all sure whether to believe you're there or not. I can see you and hear you, but maybe it's my liver acting up again. I've certainly never come up against a dead Indian before. It's not the sort of thing you expect in London though goodness knows what's going to happen next with all the foreigners around the place. What are the neighbors going to think if I have an Indian in my flat?"

"But they can't see me, as I've pointed out before, so they won't know I'm there," he replied. "Look. Why don't you just let me come along and explain everything when you get home? It's no good talking here because as I said people will think you're talking to yourself."

This last was true. A policeman who had been watching Mrs. Searwood from under the brim of his helmet sauntered over.

"Anything I can do for you, ma'am?" he asked. "Oh, it's you, Mrs. Searwood. Not lost your key again, I hope?"

"No," said Mrs. Searwood, whose trouble with keys added to her conviction that one person walking down the street with a flashlight didn't destroy a blackout was one of the minor tribulations of the Westminster police station. "No. I haven't lost my key, officer. I was just thinking out loud." Then to the Indian, "You can come home if you promise to behave." The policeman looked at her with mild shock and walked firmly and pointedly off in the other direction.

"Bother," said Mrs. Searwood, "it's dreadfully difficult talking to someone who isn't there with somebody else there. I mean talking to someone who is there really but who— Oh, never mind. Come along."

Mrs. Searwood's flat was at the top of Hakluyt House—a six-story building containing some hundred apartments and situated a block from the Thames. Hakluyt House had been built in the early twenties as "a garden home situated in the very heart of London, for discriminating guests." The older residents called it the Barracks, for it had been laid out by an architect with an adoration for uniformity. The building was meticulously square, the garden being enclosed in the square center court. The garden was square too. It had square flower beds with a square lawn, as austere as the top of a bridge table, around them. Mrs. Searwood had decided to live at Hakluyt House because she was fond of gardens, but somehow the flowers, planted perforce in squares in the flower beds of the same uncompromising shape, had taken on a kind of squareness for her. She had, during the early days of her tenancy, suggested that a path be cut through the lawn to facilitate passing from one side of the garden to the other. She hoped that this would produce two oblongs by way of variety. But the management had cut not one path, but two, bisecting each other to a nicety. Instead of two oblongs four squares resulted. After that she had given up. She rarely went into the garden, and when her daughter Priscilla had asked her once why she didn't spend more time there, Mrs. Searwood had replied that she was afraid she might see a square bird. Priscilla did not understand and was worried about the reply for some time.

Self-service elevators carried the guests at Hakluyt House to their various floors, but Mrs. Searwood didn't trust them because she had an abiding fear of any machine that ran itself. She considered that such machines were getting too intelligent and if people continued to patronize them, they might one day become smarter than human beings and obtain the mastery. So she always plodded up the six flights of stairs, as she did now, pausing at each landing to get her breath.

Her flat, of as geometrical a design as the whole building, consisted of a bed-sitting room, a tiny kitchen and a bathroom. It contained all that was left of her household furnishings, the remnants of two bombings in what she felt was a personal war between herself and Hitler. There was a mahogany secretary, with a glass-fronted bookcase at the back of it, a teak chest from India across which gamboled some plump Eastern nudes, a handsome straight-backed chair, a small side table (with extension) of dark oak in the Jacobean style, and an armchair. The rest of her belongings she had stored in a warehouse at Brighton on the advice of her daughter Priscilla. The warehouse two days later had suffered a direct bomb hit and as a result of this and other occurrences of an unwarrantably hostile nature Mrs. Searwood was convinced that Hitler had an especial grudge against her.

"I was in Berlin in 1935 and I said then that I thought the Germans were a dirty lot, and that's what did it," she would explain. And when people looked askance at such a pronouncement, she would add, "The Gestapo, you know. Secret police."

It was Mrs. Searwood's habit when disturbed to make a cup of tea, and this she did now, setting out two cups on a tray with some diluted powdered milk in a small silvered jug.

"No sugar, I'm afraid, and only that kind of milk that they took the milk out of to help the war effort," she said. "Or perhaps you can't drink tea?"

"No," replied the Indian. "One of the nice things about being dead is that you're never hungry or thirsty but always in a state of being just comfortably full. You can choose your own flavor for the fullness too. I prefer roast beef. But go ahead. I'm quite used to sitting down and taking nothing."

He waited until she was seated in her chair—the easy one—and then sat down on a sofa that served as a bed at nighttime.

"You've heard, I suppose," he said, "of Pocahontas?"

"I think so," said Mrs. Searwood. "He's a Russian general."

The Indian gulped.

"No," he replied, "Pocahontas was an Indian princess who married an Englishman by the name of Rolfe. He brought her from America to London where she was received by the King and made a great deal of fuss over. She was unable to adjust herself to the English climate and caught pneumonia during the winter and died."

"Poor thing," said Mrs. Searwood, "The fuel rationing is really terrible. I usually stoke up the fire on Monday evenings and then the rest of the week arrange to visit friends who haven't used up their coal. It can be done if you plan it and play gin rummy. Still, you'd have thought the government would have stretched a point or two for an American princess in the interest of Anglo-American relations. Strange that I didn't see anything about it in the papers, but then they don't print all the news these days."

"This," said the Indian with enormous restraint, "was in the year 1617 when James I was on the throne. Long before you were born."

"Well, it is a very interesting story," said Mrs. Searwood not a whit disturbed, "but I don't see what it's got to do with you waiting for a bus with practically nothing on."

"It has everything to do with me waiting for a bus with practically nothing on," replied the Indian. "It explains why I am here. I was one of the tribe of Pocahontas and was assigned by her father to accompany her to England and to watch over her. He said that if any harm came to her at all, I would be held personally responsible for it and he would probably beat out my brains with a stone club. So when she died, I decided to stay on in England. And when

I died, which was ten years later, I had got so attached to the place that I stayed anyway.

"It's a peculiar position to be in, you'll have to agree. I'm a displaced Indian. I became so interested in watching what was going on here that I didn't want to leave for the happy hunting grounds of my ancestors, where my reception might be somewhat less than cordial. And then I came to realize that I could never be content there anyway—knowing all I do about philosophy, history, nuclear physics, differential calculus, organic chemistry, botany, zoology and so on. All my ancestors would seem so simple to me, and I just couldn't spend an eternity with people who, even if they are my relatives, are essentially ignorant, if not downright barbarous."

"You mean that you're an educated man?" exclaimed Mrs. Searwood in surprise.

"Certainly," replied the Indian. "I've graduated no less than two hundred and sixty-one times *magna cum laude* from Oxford University and fourteen times from Cambridge. Of course, neither of them gave me a degree although I attended all the lectures in every course of study offered. They could hardly give a degree to a disembodied spirit. But I am master of all the learning available at the two most honored universities in England. I've read every volume in the library of the British Museum, and I speak every tongue known to man with the exception of such languages as Mayan and Aztec which, thanks to the civilizing influence of the Western world, have been lost completely for all time."

"Good gracious," said Mrs. Searwood, "you really are a remarkable man."

"Thank you," said the Indian.

"But tell me—why did you decide to pick on me to haunt?"

"I reject the inference that I am haunting you," the Indian said with a tinge of annoyance. "Haunting is a pastime of only the lowest grades of spirits, and as you yourself have admitted, I'm a spirit of some distinction. Haunting compares with the affectations of the more vulgar types of human beings, who are never happy unless they are calling attention to themselves. Rattling chains and banging doors and so on. Utter nonsense. I prefer to think that I am guiding and counseling you, since that was my intention. You recall the airplanes?"

"I certainly do," said Mrs. Searwood.

"Well, that is but one example of the many ways in which I can be of service to you. I can keep you constantly informed of anything in the way of bombs that is coming your way, and I can offer you the companionship of a man who is by no means a clod when it comes to conversation.

"As a matter of fact that was my intention in introducing myself to you in the first instance—or deciding to haunt you as you so unhappily put it."

"But why did you pick on me out of the millions of people in London?"

"Sentiment," replied the Indian. "When I came to London in 1616 I never lacked for company. There were people constantly coming to see me, day and night. In fact, they hardly gave me a moment to myself. But when I had learned the language I soon discovered that they had not come to talk *to* me so much as to examine me and talk *about* me afterwards. If I had had two heads, I couldn't have been a greater curiosity. I was the butt of a hundred jokes of an uncomplimentary nature—many of the stories told today about Scotsmen, Irishmen, traveling salesmen and so on were originated around myself. The result of all this was that I was lonely in the extreme. After Princess Pocahontas died, I had no companionship at all until a certain Mistress Plumpton—an ancestor of yours—took pity on me and allowed me to stay at the Sign of the Bear and Ragged Staff of which she was the proprietress. We developed a friendship of a strictly respectable nature which lasted the rest of my life.

"When I saw you standing by the bus stop, I was struck with the likeness between you and your ancestor, and overcome with a certain nostalgia. I suspected that you were lonely. So I decided to introduce myself to you and materialized for your especial benefit."

He paused and then continued. "I trust that this explanation will show that my intentions were of the best. There was one further and rather selfish reason for my action, however, of which I must tell you in all honesty. The fact is that I've been getting somewhat lonely myself recently. The constant bombardments and disturbance of the atmosphere by planes of all kinds, flying at high speeds, have driven most of the spirits out of London. It is extremely hard to keep one's ectoplasm intact under such conditions. I believe that at the present time I am the only spirit left in this city. I felt the need of companionship and, recalling my early and rewarding friendship with your progenitor, decided to introduce myself to you. However, if it is your wish, I shall retire without intruding further."

Mrs. Searwood poured herself another cup of tea and contemplated the Indian. "To tell you the truth," she said, "I was a wee bit lonely, though I don't like to let on about it to anybody. It's the war really. When it started, everything was different. People I hadn't spoken to in years of living in this apartment house became fast friends in a week. We gave teas and shelter parties and sewing bees and took air-raid drill and did all sorts of things together. It's funny when you think of it, but it was only the fear of dying that made us enjoy living together as people.

"But the war has been going on for five years now and the novelty has gone long ago. We all got used to it and have gone back to our old ways of preferring privacy to friendliness. We've become little islands again, living in a big island. All my old friends have moved out of London long ago and the new residents are busy with their jobs. And blackouts are an awful hindrance to visiting. So lately I've been alone quite a lot. Just before I met you, as a matter of fact, I'd been thinking to myself how much I would like to have an American friend like some of the neighbors do . . . though of course I didn't expect a ghost."

"Spirit," corrected the Indian. "Ghosts are just a vulgar superstition."

"Well, I wasn't expecting a spirit. But since you're here, I must say I think I'm rather pleased about it. Particularly since you can talk. What is your name, by the way?"

"Chief White Feather, Doctor of Music, Doctor of Law, Doctor of Medicine, Doctor of Philosophy, Doctor of Art, Doctor of Science,

Doctor of Divinity, etc., etc. Sometimes I forget the different branches of learning in which I excel."

"I shan't be able to talk to you much about that kind of thing," Mrs. Searwood said. "If you don't mind my saying so, I'm not at all sure that learning is much good anyway. Of course, I've got nothing against people going to universities and studying if they've got nothing better to do, as in your case. But you've got to have a good deal of ignorance around to elect a government. If everybody was devoted to knowledge they'd hesitate to express an opinion in a ballot lest they be wrong, and popular government would be impossible. Furthermore, I've found that exceptionally well-educated people constantly differ with each other, but others agree on things quite readily, I suppose because they've got housework and things like that to attend to."

"Madam," said Chief White Feather, "you have uncovered the whole secret of electing a government by ballot. A thesis on the subject would win you a degree in political science."

"I don't want a degree in political science," replied Mrs. Searwood. "All I want is the end of the war and a new girdle. And it's my belief that the whole world wants about the same thing."

CHAPTER THREE

PRISCILLA BRENTLY, Mrs. Searwood's only daughter, had had from early childhood an all-embracing sense of responsibility and a truly awful drive for organizing. It is only fair to record that she was a goodhearted woman and it is possible that her urge to take care of people and things and pat them into tidy shapes like cubes of butter sprung from her goodheartedness. Nonetheless she was a woman to be reckoned with and to keep at a distance if any personal initiative was to be retained, and it was for this reason that Mrs. Searwood had insisted on getting an apartment of her own when her husband died ten years previously.

At first she had thought of moving in with her daughter and son-in-law. But some instinct for self-preservation had asserted itself and given her the strength to resist their offers. For Mrs. Searwood was just the opposite of her daughter, and she was frequently mildly surprised that she should have mothered such a domineering and order-conscious offspring. Mrs. Searwood disliked things being organized and tidy and had gone through life happily dropping newspapers on the floor and letting them lie there, forgetting to return books to the library, sweeping dust under the carpets and locking herself out of her apartment.

"You can't organize comfort," she would say. "The two are opposed to each other and natural enemies."

All this laxness, she knew, would be forbidden her if she moved in with Priscilla. And so she had refused to do so and taken her own apartment at Hakluyt House.

The result was a kind of uneasy truce. Priscilla had a habit of dropping in on a sort of superintendent's tour of inspection to see whether her mother and her apartment were tidy and properly regulated. And Mrs. Searwood had for her own peace of mind developed an emergency drill for such occasions. This consisted of a flurried scooping of everything in sight into the broom cupboard, flinging open the window (for Priscilla was a great believer in fresh air, however inclement the weather) and hurriedly wiping the tops of the furniture with a cloth which she kept for such emergencies behind one of the cushions of the easy chair.

Priscilla came around to see her mother now on one of her inspection tours. She had had a thoroughly successful day from her point of view. She had given a demonstration on making curtains out of old sacks to the housewives on her street, had instructed the mothers of a troop of Girl Guides on their duties at next Sunday's outings, had arranged for each girl to bring two sandwiches and a bottle of cold tea and meet her at Queen's Park Gate; had found twelve bottles for girls who said they couldn't find any bottles; obtained flowers for the Sunday service at church; told three mothers what to do about three separate ailments of three separate children, and still had half an hour's organizing to spare before returning home and making her husband's dinner.

At her knock, three raps of such precision and force as to be unmistakable for any other, Mrs. Searwood swept the *Times*, the *Observer*, the *Picture Post*, a tiny fragment of butter, two teacups and an ash tray into the cupboard, waved her hand a few times in the air to dissipate the tobacco smoke, flung up the window, wiped off the furniture and ordered the astonished Indian into the broom cupboard too.

"It's Priscilla," she hissed, "my daughter. She mustn't find you here."

"She can't see me," Chief White Feather protested.

"She can see everything," said Mrs. Searwood. "Hurry and don't break the teacups."

"I won't go," said White Feather.

"Please," pleaded Mrs. Searwood in a panic at the delay, "I tell you Priscilla even sees things that aren't there." The Indian melted into the broom cupboard reluctantly, flowing over a collection of mops, feather dusters, floor polish, china and buckets with obvious disgust.

"Come in, dear," said Mrs. Searwood nervously, tucking her hair into place. Priscilla entered. She was dressed in a well-tailored grey worsted suit and was wearing a yellow sweater, for although it was early May the day had been cold and overcast. Her shoes, while handsome and of good quality, had a vague suggestion about them of golf and long walks. She was a woman in her early thirties, blue-eyed, fresh-complexioned, her straight eyebrows paralleled by a straight mouth which conveyed the impression that after Gibraltar had been washed away, Priscilla would still be there, and not very wet either.

"Hello darling," she said, dabbed a greeting with her lips on Mrs. Searwood's cheek, and sat down in the straight-backed chair.

"Hello," said Mrs. Searwood, one eye on the broom closet.

"Is there anything wrong?" asked Priscilla, sensing her mother's distraction. "I thought I heard you talking to someone while I was outside the door. You haven't picked yourself up a handsome young American, have you?"

Mrs. Searwood started and commenced to color.

"Certainly not," she said, "what a preposterous idea. I was just talking to myself by accident. You know how it is. You want to say something to somebody that you forgot to tell them the last time you saw them, and it bothers you so much that you say it out loud. Of course, you forget to say it next time you meet them too, but at least you've had the satisfaction of saying it to yourself . . ." Mrs. Searwood's voice trailed off with the sentence incomplete. She was conscious that she was talking what her daughter regarded as non-sense, though she found it perfectly sensible herself.

"Well," she ended lamely, "I was just talking to myself."

"Mother," said Priscilla abruptly, "I've been thinking about you."

"Oh dear," said Mrs. Searwood. Long experience had taught her that there was some unpleasant piece of organizing coming up when Priscilla used that tone.

"Yes," continued Priscilla, "I've been thinking about you and it seems to me that it's not good for you to be here all alone. It just isn't right for elderly people to be alone. After a life of companionship, busy with their families and their friends, solitude is bad for them. They need someone around to take care of them and provide some company."

Mrs. Searwood felt a mounting sense of desperation. This was an old theme of Priscilla's and one which she returned to more often recently. Mrs. Searwood was normally docile with her daughter, pretending to fall in with her suggestions. But she knew that this was something on which to be firm while there was still an opportunity to make a stand.

"I don't see how you can say that," she said. "Until you're an elderly person yourself, you can't possibly know what elderly people want. There are too many people trying to make elderly people do things that they think they would do if they were elderly people but if they were, that is elderly people, I mean, they wouldn't want to do them at all." She was conscious that the thread of argument had got rather badly knotted in that sentence, but went on anyway. "Besides," she continued, "I'm perfectly happy as I am and completely able to take care of myself. You know, I took care of you once, though it surprises me to realize this now. You just happened to come in at a time when I was talking to myself, but there really isn't any harm in that. I never quarrel with myself and indeed take a great deal of pleasure in my own conversation. If I had someone else around I'd have to keep agreeing with them when I didn't want to, so as to avoid quarrels. You know, you don't have to adjust yourself to yourself, but you do have to adjust yourself to other people and I think that's what's responsible for all these nervous breakdowns." Mrs. Searwood paused, conscious of the limning of a great idea. "Society would be all right if it weren't for other people," she said emphatically.

"Hear! Hear!" cried Chief White Feather from the broom cupboard.

"You keep quiet. I don't need any advice from you," said Mrs. Searwood, cutting off her daughter who had just opened her mouth to say something.

"Why Mother!" exclaimed Priscilla, "whatever has got into you? I've never heard you go on so strangely before. You used to be so docile and sweet."

"Tell her you've grown up and achieved an age of reason," said White Feather.

"I've grown up and achieved an age of reason," said Mrs. Searwood. She did not say it because she wanted to say it, but because she had, under Priscilla's domination, developed a habit of repeating what she was told to repeat.

"Well," said Priscilla with such emphasis that she might have invented the word herself, "I must say that this is a fine way to act when your daughter calls around to see how you are. I spend a great deal of time thinking and worrying about you, Mother, and so does Peter." (Peter was Priscilla's husband and was always dragged in for reinforcement to turn the tide in any discussion. This was because Mrs. Searwood had once said she had a great deal of admiration for Peter, though Priscilla hadn't understood the reason why she said so.)

"What I wanted to say if you'll give me a chance—and Peter feels exactly the same way as I do—is that it's not good for you to be here all alone at night-times. You're just not yourself and your present attitude certainly justifies that conclusion. I decided—Peter and I—that it would be much better for you, and would relieve our own minds into the bargain, if you left London for a time and went to stay in the country. There would be an easier life for you altogether there and more companionship. And you know, Mother, you can't always be lucky about bombs. People do get killed by them."

"Don't tell me about bombs," said Mrs. Searwood, "after that man Hitler blew up all my furniture. I knew the very day that your father brought home that one-year clock under the glass dome that something dreadful was going to happen to it. It really relieved my mind when it went up in smithereens."

"Mother," said Priscilla gently, "we were talking about your going to the country."

"I know we were," replied Mrs. Searwood, "and I don't want to leave here. I feel much safer in London. The police know me and are always nice to me and the Houses of Parliament are near by so that if anything serious goes wrong I can always call on somebody in a position of responsibility to get something done about it."

"You haven't been going over to Parliament with your problems?" asked Priscilla in alarm. "You promised faithfully that you wouldn't do anything like that. You know, Parliament isn't there to look after individual people, but the nation as a whole."

"The nation as a whole is made up of individual people and you can't separate one from the other," retorted Mrs. Searwood primly. "But you needn't worry. I kept my promise. All I did was when they cut off the gas between four and six in the afternoon just when I was getting dinner ready, I called up the Minister of Fuel and told him to have it turned on again . . ."

"Oh no, Mother!" wailed Priscilla, "you didn't do that, surely? They cut off the gas between those hours for the whole of London. It wasn't just you. It was everybody—to save fuel."

"Well then, why didn't everybody object to it instead of leaving it to an old woman like me? You know the trouble with government is that there are too many people relying on too few to do too much for them."

"You've hit the nail right on the head," said Chief White Feather. He opened the door of the broom closet and waved a feather duster in the air in his enthusiasm. Since the broom cupboard was behind the chair in which Priscilla was sitting, she didn't see it, but the look of horror on her mother's face caused her to turn around. The feather duster disappeared in the nick of time.

"What *is* the matter with you, Mother?" Priscilla demanded.

"Nothing, dear. I thought I saw some feathers floating around by your head, but it must be my glasses."

"You haven't got your glasses on," said Priscilla. "I don't see any feathers."

"You'd get a horrid shock if you did," said White Feather.

"Look, Mother," continued Priscilla, "this about settles it. This being alone is getting you down. A trip to the country is just what you need. Peter and I have picked out a nice little cottage fully furnished in Lower Pupton le Soeur just outside Winchester. It's a lovely little village and we've arranged for a housekeeper who does for the vicar to come in and do all your cooking and housework. There's a wonderful garden for you to grow things in. It will do you a world of good and it's all arranged for you to leave on the afternoon train tomorrow from Victoria. Why don't you give it a trial? The air will make a new woman of you, there'll be lots of fresh vegetables, and you'll probably be able to get an extra egg or two a week. If you don't like it, you can come right back. We'll keep the flat for you—that's a promise."

Mrs. Searwood hesitated. She had thought all along that what Priscilla was going to propose was some kind of home for elderly ladies, and it was a relief to be told that that wasn't the case at all. She liked eggs and she loved gardening, but there were still drawbacks. She had lived in a village once before and had come away with some mixed views on rural living. There were many attractions; lots and lots of things to gossip about, the garden, and the importance which attaches to every movement you make being reported to everyone else in the community.

But it was the water problem that made her hesitate chiefly. The last time she had lived in a country house, she had discovered that the plumbing had apparently been designed with the express purpose of preventing bathing. There had been water laid on to the house, it was true. It came from a storage tank outside which had been put below the level of the kitchen floor. To get any water into the kitchen, it had to be pumped by hand.

By an inspired piece of misdesigning, the bathroom was upstairs. When you turned on the faucet in the bath it roared and gurgled quite frighteningly, spewed out a trickle of brown liquid and then relapsed into a boding silence. Sometimes it would roar again just as you were going out of the door. All this was the signal for more hand pumping downstairs. You pumped away for half an hour to raise the water to the upstairs tank. Then you waited for an hour for it to heat enough for a bath. Someone else frequently came and took the bath before you.

With this experience in mind, Mrs. Searwood decided that she would not go to Lower Pupton le Soeur.

"Nobody in the country ever washes themselves," she said, "and at my age I'm not going to live among a lot of soiled people. Unless this cottage has hot and cold water laid on, and some method of getting it into the bathtub other than in buckets, I shan't stir a foot out of here."

"We've looked into everything," assured Priscilla, "and there's a modern water heater in the cottage and an electric pump, so there'll even be more hot water than you get in London."

Mrs. Searwood was still dubious.

"What about air-raid shelters?" she asked.

"Don't be ridiculous, Mother," said Priscilla. "The Germans are not going to interrupt the war to bomb a little English village."

"That's just where you're wrong," said Mrs. Searwood. "You forget about my visit to Berlin and my saying that the Germans were dirty people and the secret police marking it down in their little notebooks. They've been after me from the word go. I wouldn't feel safe at all unless there was an air-raid shelter."

"Well, there's an Anderson in the garden with some potted geraniums in it, and the house has a huge brick cellar which is better than most shelters around here. So you'll be perfectly safe. You won't even have to go down a lot of stairs to get to it."

After some more argument, Mrs. Searwood finally agreed, with some reservations, to give Lower Pupton a trial.

"Well, that's settled then," said Priscilla with a sigh. She gathered her things together in a hurry, for she was late, and said as she left, "I'll be back to help you pack after I've given Peter his dinner."

As she walked down the corridor to the elevator, there was a piercing wolf whistle and she turned around, startled, to see her mother peering after her from the doorway.

"Really, Mother," said Priscilla.

"Drat that Indian," muttered Mrs. Searwood and closed the door.

CHAPTER FOUR

LOWER PUPTON LE SOEUR lies in a fold of chalk hills, five miles outside of Winchester. The hills slide gently upward until they merge with the tableland of the Hampshire Downs. The village, though it has for the most part lived gently and in peace through the centuries, has now and then slowly and almost with a sigh, had to put aside its work and go to war. Its history mirrors in miniature that of the whole nation from Roman times, through the Saxons, Danes and Normans and on to the establishment of empire.

Every now and then there would be a call to Lower Pupton from such places as Winchester in the early days and then London, for the menfolk to take up arms. And they took the bow from the chimney corner or the rifle from the Army quartermaster according to the period and went out to fight Saracen or Frenchman, Spaniard or Dutchman, German or Fuzzy Wuzzy in places as far apart as the Holy Land and the Khyber Pass. At the end of each such engagement, the men trickled back with their trophies—Saracen shields or German helmets—and undisturbed by the sights they had seen returned to their old ways.

For the people of the village, Lower Pupton was England, and if they had any formulated policy for the nation and for themselves, it was that progress was a degenerative evil, certain to reduce men to manikins and utterly destroy their institutions. So life in the village remained basically unchanged through the centuries, its ploughs drawn by horses, its harvest carried in carts made by the village carpenter, its cottages roofed by the village thatcher and its rents collected by the village bailiff.

Mrs. Searwood liked Lower Pupton as soon as she saw it, despite the fact that the Southern Railway had no depot nearer than Winchester, and she had had to take a bus the remainder of the way. For one thing, the heavily thatched roofs looked so pretty as the bus came over the crest of Cobb's Folly to reveal the village below. And then each cottage had a garden with the promise of summer hollyhocks and sunflowers, snapdragons and Sweet Williams. There was a pond at the threshold of the village in which cattle and horses watered and Mrs. Searwood thought that very picturesque too, though she had a flutter of misgiving wondering whether the water for her cottage would be drawn from the same pond.

"I don't like the idea of horses spitting in my bath water," she said to Chief White Feather. Mrs. Manners, who was sitting behind her and whose husband ran the only grocery store in Lower Pupton, came at this point to the unalterable conclusion that Mrs. Searwood was a bomb-shock victim from London and probably out of her mind.

All the way from Winchester, Mrs. Manners had been wondering who Mrs. Searwood might be. It was quite unusual for strangers to travel on the Lower Pupton bus and her interest had been pinched from the moment that Mrs. Searwood's enormous quantity of bags and hatboxes had been put aboard at the Butter Cross in Winchester. She had got what glimpse she could of those bags, and even in such haphazard examination as was possible in the time the bags were put on the bus, had discovered Mrs. Searwood's name and the fact (betrayed by some ancient labels) that she had been in Germany.

This had immediately aroused in Mrs. Manners's active mind the theory, amounting for fully five minutes to a conviction, that Mrs. Searwood was a German spy. She had reluctantly relinquished this because it didn't seem probable that German spies would be walking about England with German labels on their baggage. She had then concluded that Mrs. Searwood was a British subject who had been resident in Germany when the war broke out and who had just managed to get home. But she was too plump for that. Everybody knew that the Germans were eating sawdust instead of bread and sausage, and the whole nation wasting away except Goering who was getting fatter. She toyed with the idea that Mrs. Searwood was a secret agent of the British government who displayed German labels on her baggage in order to attract the attention of sympathizers with the Nazi cause and so uncover them. That theory lasted her for fifteen minutes and would have been spread through the village in five more when she got there. And then Mrs. Searwood had spoken aloud to herself saying, "I don't like the idea of horses spitting in my bath water." So it was evident, beyond all contesting, that Mrs. Searwood was a shock victim, and the matter of the German labels would have to be investigated later.

The bus now rumbled to a stop in the main street of the village outside a half-timbered inn called the Fox and Hounds. Mrs. Searwood got off, with Mrs. Manners so anxious not to be separated from her that she nearly fell down the steps.

"I see you're staying in Lower Pupton," said Mrs. Manners. "That's nice. What house are you going to?"

"The Yews," replied Mrs. Searwood.

"That's right on my way," said Mrs. Manners. "I'll be glad to take you there, if you like, and help with the bags." Mrs. Searwood thanked her, Mrs. Manners picked up two of the bags after a hard glance at the labels, and they set off together. Chief White Feather falling in behind said to Mrs. Searwood, "This biddy probably gives out a regular broadcast like the BBC. Be careful what you say to her."

"I've nothing to say to her anyway," said Mrs. Searwood.

Mrs. Manners gave her a quick and frightened look. She was shocked because she had been speculating on how she could get Mrs. Searwood to tell her something of herself without appearing nosy, and Mrs. Searwood seemed to have read her thoughts. She decided Mrs. Searwood was probably psychic. Lots of people were.

"Real nice house, the Yews," she said. She looked like a sparrow that had somehow put on a woman's clothes. She wore a hat reminiscent of the flapper days and had a trim of fur around her overcoat. "It's got a dining room and a living room downstairs, and two bedrooms upstairs and a nice bathroom. Don't pay any attention at night if the stairs creak. That's only Old Grady."

"Old Grady?" exclaimed Mrs. Searwood. "My daughter told me I was to have the place to myself. I wasn't expecting to share it with someone."

"Old Grady won't bother you," said Mrs. Manners, "he's a ghost. Hanged himself in the Yews in Nollie Cromwell's time. At least that's what the village talk is. Of course I don't put much stock in it myself. Still, if the stairs creak, just shut your bedroom door tight and get under the covers."

"I'll do nothing of the sort," said Mrs. Searwood. "I'll go right out and tell him to stop his noise."

"You leave him to me," said Chief White Feather, "I'll put an end to his nonsense."

"That's right," said Mrs. Searwood, "throw him out."

"Did you say something?" asked Mrs. Manners, who was getting uneasy about Mrs. Searwood's habit of soliloquy.

"I was just talking to myself," explained Mrs. Searwood and then, in case she made any further slips, she added, "I do it quite a lot, I'm afraid."

The Yews lay back in its own grounds off the village street. It was something more than a cottage or even a house and yet not big enough to be called a manor house. A hedge of yew cut it off from the road, and the front lawn, bright after the spring rain, was patterned with flower beds in which stood clusters of daffodils and spikes of narcissus. Mrs. Searwood noted with delight that the flower beds were circular and lozenge-shaped, and liked the garden right away.

Mrs. Skipton, who was to do for Mrs. Searwood, answered her knock. She was a fat, jolly-looking woman whose reddened arms conveyed the impression that she had just baked several batches of loaves in a hot oven.

"Mrs. Searwood?" she asked in a pleasant voice. "Come right in. I've got everything ready for you. Thank you very much, Mrs. Manners. So nice of you to come out of your way to bring Mrs.

Searwood here. Would you stop by at the baker and ask them to start leaving the bread in the morning?" Mrs. Manners had hoped to be able to stay a little while and find out more about the intriguing new arrival. But there was a note of dismissal in the last sentence that could not be ignored, and so she left. Mrs. Skipton showed Mrs. Searwood into a pleasant living room whose comfortable chairs and sofa were covered in a faded flowered cretonne.

"I'm Mrs. Skipton," she said, "and I'll be doing for you. Breakfast in the morning and then back in the afternoon to tidy and make dinner. Mrs. Manners is a nice person but she has her ways and you mustn't put too much stock in what she says. She's one of those spiritualists, you know. Always seeing people who aren't there and hearing voices that don't come over the wireless. Did she say anything to you about the house?" The question was put a little too diffidently.

"Well," said Mrs. Searwood, "she said there was someone called Old Grady who keeps walking up the stairs at nighttime."

"Not a word of truth in it," said Mrs. Skipton with emphasis. "Just village gossip."

"Oh, I don't mind really," said Mrs. Searwood. She was going to say that she was getting quite used to spirits, but Chief White Feather put his fingers to his lips to caution her.

"Who is or was this Old Grady anyway?" she asked.

"Well, in Oliver Cromwell's time, he's supposed to have worked in a tavern which stood on this site. There are still some remnants of the old building to be found in the house. He betrayed some Cavalier to the Roundheads in return for a reward of twenty pounds, and when he had spent the money he began to feel bad about it and hanged himself and good riddance. The villagers say that his ghost haunts the place, looking for the Cavalier so he can tell him he's sorry and beg his forgiveness. But that's just a story to frighten children. Don't you put any stock in it. And now I expect you'd like a cup of tea before looking around. I'm afraid I'll have to leave you after showing you through the house but I'll be back again to fix dinner after I've been over to the parson's."

"Who is the parson?" asked Mrs. Searwood.

"Reverend Lawrence Pendlebury—Low Church," said Mrs. Skipton. "He lives in the two-story house at the top of Cobb's Folly—that's the hill you came down on the bus. He's an elderly man and a bachelor and a little lonely." She eyed Mrs. Searwood speculatively and excused herself.

"I don't like the way she said that," said Mrs. Searwood.

"Just tentative matchmaking," said Chief White Feather, stretching out on the couch before the brick fireplace. "There's nothing so interests some women as trying to marry other women off. She probably knows already that you're a widow and has the whole thing worked out."

"A preposterous suggestion," retorted Mrs. Searwood, going to the mirror and touching her soft white hair into place with her hands. She conceded to herself that she was not really what you could call old-looking. There was still a touch of freshness to her fair skin and her blue eyes were not unattractive, particularly when she took off her glasses.

Chief White Feather watched the little performance with a smile. "My remarks are based on several hundred years of first-hand observation of women," he said. "I think it might pay off for me to go and have a look at the parson before a formal introduction between you two is effected."

"You stay right here while I have my tea," retorted Mrs. Searwood. "My goodness, you carry on like a romantic schoolgirl with your notions. Besides, I won't have you frightening the parson. And anyway, I want someone to talk to and help me find things around this place."

CHAPTER FIVE

THE DISCOVERY that the Yews had a ghost of its own annoyed Mrs. Searwood and she made no bones about it to Chief White Feather as she sipped her tea in the living room of her new home.

"It's a pretty harsh thing when a woman comes to my age and finds herself the center of attraction of the whole spirit world," she said. "Not that I mind you, for I have got used to having you around. Besides, you're someone to talk to. But this other man that hanged himself—I don't like the idea of him at all. I've half a mind to go back to London tonight. I'd sooner face Priscilla than have a former suicide walking up and down my stairs at nighttime."

"There isn't a train back to London until tomorrow," said Chief White Feather, "so there's nothing you can do about it now. Besides, you may find this man quite as entertaining as myself. Not many people have been able to interview a suicide after the act— indeed I don't know of anyone who can claim to have done so. You may learn something very instructive indeed. The very nature of suicide, while it stirs up widespread speculation and a whole host of theories, prohibits any serious and reliable conclusions on the state of mind and motives involved since the principal and sole witness, as it were, is unable to testify.

"In England it is customary in such cases to return a verdict of suicide while of unsound mind. I suspect, however, that this is often merely a sop to the people who don't commit suicide. To suggest that anyone killed themselves while sane might lead to uncomplimentary conclusions being drawn about a lot of others who persist in continuing to live.

"Actually, once you get used to it, it's very pleasant being dead, and for myself, I look forward to meeting Old Grady and having a chat with him. It's been quite a long time since I met another spirit—almost a year. Not, I hasten to add, that I find your conversation dull. Far from it. You have a nice streak of basic sense in you that would have delighted Socrates. Nonetheless one likes to talk with one's own kind now and then."

"What do you talk to each other about?" Mrs. Searwood asked, interested.

"Academic topics almost entirely," said White Feather. "At least, most of us do. You see, we wraiths are completely spiritual and that rules out the normal subjects of discussion among physical people such as food, clothing, prices, sex, anger, love and so on. The last exchange of any merit I had was with the spirit of Kit Marlowe—you remember, he's the man who taught Shakespeare the use of blank verse and was killed in a brawl at a tavern in Deptford over who would pay the bill for a night's wining and dining.

"We were discussing the human preoccupation with a search for truth. Marlowe maintained that human beings, since their basic urge is entirely towards their own comfort and happiness, resist truth by their very natures and prefer to live all their lives under a delusion, risking the most terrible consequences. There was something of this theme in his *Dr. Faustus*, you'll recall. He was able to point to a great deal of modern advertising in support of his argument, I'm afraid. He further maintained that far from seeking truth human beings flee from it, and when any of their number runs contrary to this tendency—as for example, Copernicus with his pronouncement that the world revolves around the sun, and Pasteur with his discovery concerning the sources of infection—the rest, seeing in jeopardy their precious delusions which have comforted them for hundreds of years, turn upon them like wolves and either make them recant or burn them as heretics.

"Marlowe was able to show that this aversion to truth has existed through all human history and so the sum of human knowledge is meager indeed, for, he said, humanity prefers the comforts of ignorance to the disturbance of truth because the latter demands painful adjustments.

"I had to admit that he had a good case and was delighted with his presentation of it. However, I maintained that it was the very love of truth and hatred of heresy that made mankind shun new discovery. Man, by his nature, I said, seeks to find explanations for things, and when he has found one which appears to him sound and reasonable, he guards it as the most precious of his possessions, hands it on to his sons, and holds any alternative false and dangerous since it might lead him from what is true into error.

"Thus, I said, paradoxically it is regard for truth that keeps Man in ignorance and Man lets go what he believes to be so to accept something else only with the greatest reluctance—in much the same way as he would be wary about exchanging what he held to be a diamond for a piece of glass, though what he had was in fact glass and what he was offered was a diamond. I hope I am not boring you with his kind of talk."

"Not at all," said Mrs. Searwood, "but I think people make too much fuss about establishing what they call truths and it leads to a great waste of time. I suppose we need to know some things for sure, like how to grow food and cure sickness. But it doesn't make the slightest bit of difference to me whether the sun goes round the world. I'm quite happy either way so long as it doesn't rain too much. I don't know how much time was spent in working out the right answer, but it would have been much better if they'd concentrated on finding a real cure for corns. I read somewhere that they were going to send a radio signal to Mars. That was the same day I found there wasn't a single man in the whole of the London Metropolitan Water District who could get the water pipes in my flat to stop knocking. I think it's rather silly. If scientists would find some way to take the weight out of five pounds of potatoes, I'd be glad of it.

"The truth isn't really important at all. People believe what they want to believe and if they're happier that way, then it's cruel to take their beliefs away from them. I don't know many scientists, but I've seen a lot of grocery boys. The grocery boys whistle at their work. I wonder how many scientists do. The grocery boys believe that everything will come out all right in the end. But the scientists are always telling us that something dreadful is going to happen, though it never does.

"When the experts are not telling us that we're going to run out of air, or be melted by some star that is getting hotter all the time, they talk about a better way of life in the future with all their scientific improvements, and I think that's very wrong. To believe in a better way of life, you have to be discontented with the one you have. So that all that happens is no one is ever satisfied."

"That could lead us into a discussion on happiness and whether it consists of the fulfillment of all desire or of having no desires at all to fulfill, which are two different things," said Chief White Feather. "But that takes us away from the problem of Old Grady. I don't quite know where he appears before starting his staircase-climbing stunt. He isn't around the house now or I'd have sensed his presence before. Probably he spends the daytime moping in a graveyard.

"Anyway, when he does turn up, do you want me to bring him in to you or would you prefer me to talk to him privately and get him to be reasonable about his silly haunting and call it off for the duration of your stay?"

"Well," said Mrs. Searwood dubiously, "do you think he would frighten me, or do me any harm? I don't want to be rude and refuse to see him. It seems hard, on reflection, to throw him out of a house that he's been roaming around at nighttimes for three hundred years. He has his rights, you know."

"Bless you," said Chief White Feather with a smile. "You're the only person I've met in three centuries who is prepared to admit that we spirits have rights. Everybody else, as soon as they suspect our presence, commences to exorcise us with book, bell and candle, and it's not only humiliating, it's hurtful to be so little wanted. We are not without feelings, you know.

"I'll tell you what I'll do. I'll see him first and get him to make himself presentable and caution him against making silly noises like *Oooer* and so on. And then I'll knock on the door and wait for you to admit us. It'll be less disconcerting for you than just slipping through the wall in the usual manner. I have a hunch that Old Grady will turn out to be useful, though I don't quite know in what way. I don't think he'll frighten you and it would be better to have a chat with him so that you could get to know each other. And now, if you don't mind, I'll take a stroll around the village—invisibly, of course—and see how the land lies. I'll be back by dark."

Chief White Feather slipped halfway through the wall, recollected himself, apologized, opened the door and walked out. At that moment, Mrs. Skipton returned.

"Goodness me!" she exclaimed, "I could have sworn I saw that door open and close itself."

"It was just a draft," said Mrs. Searwood quickly.

Mrs. Skipton eyed the door and then commenced to clear away the tea things.

"I managed to get a lamb chop for your dinner," she said brightly. "We're rationed on meat here like everywhere else, but it's not quite so bad if you just shut your eyes to where the meat comes from now and then. Not that I believe in depriving others, but one lamb chop isn't going to be missed. We get extra eggs too, so you can have one for breakfast if you like."

Mrs. Searwood said that she was devoted to eggs and would love a fresh one for breakfast as for the last two years she had had nothing but powdered eggs. Then she went upstairs, with Mrs. Skipton leading the way, to unpack her luggage and inspect the rest of the house.

It proved to be much larger than she had expected. Priscilla had told her it was a cottage, but there were two upstairs bedrooms of ample proportions and a bathroom, the bedrooms on one side of a corridor and the bathroom on the other. Beyond the bathroom was another small room—a boudoir for dressing in which contained a deep cupboard, dressing table and lounging chair—one of those pieces of furniture which Mrs. Searwood vaguely connected with French mistresses and Turkish harems.

"What a nice little room," she said. "Do you know, I really think I would prefer to sleep in here."

"Oh, you'll like the front bedroom much better," said Mrs. Skipton. "It's got two huge bay windows and window seats and a real four-poster bed with a feather mattress. I think you'll find it rather stuffy in here at night time."

"Was this the room that Old Grady . . . ?"

"Yes," replied Mrs. Skipton, "but I do hope you're not going to let that silly gossip bother you. I was just talking to Parson Pendlebury, who's been here for thirty years, and he said in all that time he never knew of anyone who had personally come across Old Grady. And if anybody had, the parson would know because he visits every home in the village once a week, and knows everything that's going on, though he has a most annoying way of only telling you about it months and months later."

"Men are like that," said Mrs. Searwood. "My own husband— he was a professor of agriculture—used to bore me to tears with discussions of soil analysis, but never let out a peep about the affairs of one of the dons at the university although he knew all about them, until the whole thing blew into the open on page 3 of the *News of the World*. I opened the paper one day and there it was under a heading which said 'LUST IN A LATIN CLASS' or something like that. 'George,' I said, 'what's all this?' and showed him the paper. 'Oh that,' he said, 'nothing at all. Everybody's known about it for months.' I could have brained him."

"I understand," said Mrs. Skipton, "men are always trying to protect us from the things that give us pleasure. Still I do pick up an odd item from Parson Pendlebury now and again. The Briggs boy (they live down the street and it's said they come from gypsy people who settled here about six hundred years ago—they *are* a bit strange) the Briggs boy is going to be made a flight sergeant in the RAF, and is going steady with a girl from Winchester. If that's true, it's the first time he's been steady in his life, for he's been in and out of trouble ever since the time he set fire to a hayrick when he was three.

"Then the Wedges—they're an old couple who live at the tennis court—it's really a house but we call it the tennis court—they've taken in two war orphans from London and Mrs. Wedge says its unbelievable the language they use. They were quiet enough the first day or two, but then they came running into the kitchen one day and said the biggest bloody sparrow (they used the word too) they'd ever seen had chased them down the lane and they wanted a chopper to chop off his head. Of course they were talking about the tom turkey. It is rather vicious. But the language they used. Mrs. Wedge washed their mouths out with soap and they went round telling people she was trying to poison them. Poor little mites. They're twins, eight years old, but very grown up in their ways. They're the terror of the rest of the children but I think where they came from they either had to stand up for themselves or be pushed to the wall. They've made a big change in Mr. Wedge. He was always so solemn and quiet, but since the twins came, he's been going around talkative and happy and the other day he told the postman that he thought he would adopt them because it did him good to hear someone call a spade a bloody shovel. Used the exact words.

"Mrs. Green—she's the carpenter's wife—is expecting her tenth with her ninth only three months old. She's Welsh, you know, and they say they're pretty vigorous. And Admiral Gudgeon—he lives up at the top of the village near the Old Barn—he's all upset about a piece he read in the paper saying that Gracie Fields or someone had given a piano to the men on one of the battleships. I don't know which one. But he says the Navy has gone soft and they're going to have to fall back on men like him any day now to put some iron back into it. He's retired you know though he served with Beatty in the last war, and still thinks he's spry.

"His granddaughter's in the Wrens and I don't think he likes it, for he warns her never to trust a sailor. Admiral to cabin boy, he says, they're all dangerous and maybe he's right. I think it's those bell-bottom trousers they wear. Gives them a kind of a swagger. If the Admiralty would just put them in knee pants it would keep down the birth rate in every port in the world."

Mrs. Searwood agreed. She was very happy at the harvest of tidbits that was coming her way, filling up a great vacuum that had been caused by the isolation of life in her London flat.

"I really must get around and meet some of these people," she said. "I've always thought it nice to be neighborly."

"You'll get a chance on Saturday. The vicar's giving a garden party and bazaar for the benefit of war orphans, and he asked me to tell you of it and invite you to attend. He'll probably come over himself tomorrow to pay a formal call and invite you personally, but he knows I like to carry messages, so that's why he asked me to tell you about it."

Mrs. Skipton went off to cook dinner, leaving Mrs. Searwood to unpack her clothes in a state of happiness and excitement. So many people to visit and gossip with, she thought. So many things to find out. Really such a lot to do that there was no reason at all for anybody to feel lonely. And Chief White Feather to talk things over with when there was no one else around. The thought of Chief White Feather reminded her of Old Grady and angered her for a moment.

"Really," she said, "it's getting so that you either have to take places with poor plumbing and no people, or places with good plumbing and a host of ghosts. But I shan't be frightened with Chief White Feather to help me. Still, it's bad enough meeting a ghost suddenly, but waiting to meet one is worse. I think I'll have a hot bath and try to forget about it."

She went into the bathroom and turned on the outsize faucet which was marked "Hot." A stream of deathly cold water came from it. Then she turned on the other faucet marked "Cold." It coughed and gurgled and emitted a dark brown liquid.

"Oh no!" said Mrs. Searwood in dismay.

"You have to pump from downstairs," called out Mrs. Skipton. "The electric doesn't work and that water tank up there is empty so you have to pump by hand. It will take two hours to get a bath, I'm afraid."

"I know," said Mrs. Searwood wearily, "I know. Where's the pump?"

CHAPTER SIX

M<small>RS</small>. S<small>EARWOOD WROTE A LONG LETTER</small> to Priscilla on the subject of the water supply at the Yews before going to bed. It was a rambling letter dealing with the Wedges, the twins, the parson, the water, Admiral Gudgeon, the Briggs boy, Mrs. Skipton, the coming garden party, and it was only with considerable effort that she managed to leave out the comments of the shade of Kit Marlowe on the state of human ignorance. Priscilla, she decided, would not understand that.

The bed, a four-poster which had been shortened in the legs so that it could be entered without a ladder, was, she decided, the most comfortable she had ever slept in. The feather mattress was snug and soothing, the pillows plump and well stuffed, and the sheets had a gentle fragrance to them as if they had been put to air in a flower garden. Mrs. Searwood propped two of the pillows up against the headboard to settle down to an hour's reading while awaiting the arrival of Old Grady. She didn't like whodunits because she couldn't understand the way people talked in them—as if they were saying things to each other by cablegram at several shillings a word. She preferred the more leisurely authors, and had now got to the part of *Huckleberry Finn* where Huckleberry meets the Duke, and she tut-tutted to herself and chuckled as she read and now and then said out loud, "Well I never," and paused to wipe the tears of laughter from under her glasses.

She became so absorbed with the Duke's plans for a stage presentation from Shakespeare for men only that she almost forgot about Old Grady and when there was a knock on the door said absent-mindedly, "Come in," without even bothering to look up.

The door commenced to creak open and Chief White Feather's voice said sharply, "None of those cheap tricks now. Remember what I said. Just open the door without making it creak. Here, let me do it. You've probably forgotten how."

Mrs. Searwood looked up at that and saw Chief White Feather with behind him a small lugubrious man, hunched of shoulders and bent at the knees and dressed in the prim white collar, the long jacket and full breeches of Puritan England. His hair reached down to his ears where it was cropped off as straight as a hedge, his hose drooped dismally down his thin legs and his shoes appeared worn and much too big for him.

"This," said Chief White Feather, with some contempt, "is Old Grady."

Old Grady closed his eyes and opened his mouth, preparing to emit what he hoped would be a spine-tingling *Oooer* but Chief White Feather shook him and said, "Let's leave out the penny-dreadful stuff," so he bobbed swiftly instead, like a cork in water, and said, "At your service, milady."

"I found him just as he was going to begin his silly haunting" (Old Grady squirmed) "and told him to cut it out. He said he couldn't rest and had to haunt the house and I told him that was nothing but vulgar nonsense and to come up and see you. So here he is."

"How-do-you-do?" asked Mrs. Searwood. Old Grady looked so woebegone, so henpecked, as it were, by the years, that it was quite impossible to be frightened of him. Indeed, Mrs. Searwood had a suspicion that it was he who was frightened of her.

"As well as can be expected," he replied. His voice wavered and trembled and he sounded as though he was going to burst into tears at any moment. Mrs. Searwood felt genuinely sorry for him.

"There now," she said comfortingly, "you mustn't take it too hard. If you really feel that you must haunt the place, I won't stop you, but there are things that people should give up out of consideration for others and I don't think it's right to prevent a woman

of my age getting her sleep just because you hung yourself three hundred years ago. Why did you do it, by the way?"

This was Old Grady's big moment. He knew it and he tried to make the most of it. He had for three centuries been rehearsing his answer to this question, getting the whole thing in its most dramatic frame, blending horror, suspense and pathos in such a manner as to awaken a full measure of pity, interest and respect from a world that somehow didn't care much about ghosts. Added to this he particularly wanted to rebuke Chief White Feather for his contemptuous attitude towards haunting, which had been his sole solace and indeed his death's work for so long. He straightened his shoulders and stood more upright, fixing Mrs. Searwood with a look which he hoped was sepulchral. But the wrinkled hose, the basic haircut, the comic mournfulness of his face which looked like a depressed bloodhound's, were all against him. He tried though.

"I betrayed a man to his death for twenty pounds," he said. "I plunged him into eternity; removed him from the realm of mortal beings for all time. And then I was filled with remorse and so I hanged myself in a most frightful manner."

"You spent the money first, I hope," said Mrs. Searwood.

"Yes," said Old Grady, rubbing his nose on his sleeve, "on wine and song. I couldn't find any women."

"Why did you betray this man?" Mrs. Searwood asked. "I believe he was a Royalist and you look as though you were a Crophead. Did you betray him because he was your enemy?"

"In a manner of speaking, no," said Old Grady, warming to the discussion. "It was the money, m'lady. I'd worked hard all my life and never had more than two shillings together at one time and none of it to spare. And I got to thinking that I might spend the whole of my life and never get as much as a pound together to call my own—all my life done and myself worn out like an old rag and dying and not a penny for me." He sniffed and wiped his nose on his sleeve again. "So when they posted a reward for twenty pounds for this Cavalier, and I found out he was hiding in the hen house, I couldn't resist it.

"I knew I'd never get a chance at twenty pounds again if I let this go. And I knew that this Cavalier, he'd had twenty pounds many a time and fancy ribbons to his hose and a big feather in his hat. Why, I thought, he's lived ten of my lives at half my age with pretty saucy women to bundle with and blood horses to ride and pull his carriage, and kings to do him favors and the wines of France to whet his appetite. So I told myself he shouldn't begrudge me twenty pounds seeing it's my only chance to have it. Twenty pounds wouldn't buy me a coach or a seat at a king's table, nor a dance with a woman whose hands weren't rough and red with work. But twenty pounds would make me feel noble and rich for a little while. It would make me a sort of a king among the others while it lasted. I'd buy them ale and pay a fiddler and have a dance and sing with them and they'd think they misjudged me when they called me clod and find me witty and quick in my mind and say that I was really a fine fellow."

He stopped and licked his lips.

"But it wasn't like that," he continued. "They had me drunk on three flagons and robbed on four and then threw me out. And when I'd sobered up and got to thinking about how I had betrayed a man for that, and made a failure of it all, I thought of Judas and how I was just like him. So I hanged myself in a horrible manner. And I've stayed here for three centuries hoping I'd meet the spirit of the Cavalier and crave his pardon and explain to him why it was I did it. But he's never been back."

"And small wonder, in view of what happened on his last visit," said Chief White Feather. "What did they do with him?"

"Why they took him to London and struck off his head the very day I died," replied Old Grady with a touch of pleasure. "I believe it was the very hour and perhaps the very minute. We were both plunged from the mortal world at the same time."

"Mere coincidence," said White Feather. "But I'm surprised you were able to hang yourself. You seem to have bungled everything else you turned your hand to. You say you did it in a truly horrible manner. What was the precise method, pray?"

"I don't want to tell," said Old Grady sulkily.

"Probably didn't hang himself at all," said Chief White Feather to Mrs. Searwood. "More likely he got thoroughly besotted, fell down the cellar steps and broke his head."

"Oh no I didn't," retorted Old Grady. "I know them cellar steps well. You forget I was a potman here. I hung myself by my feet so as to frighten people and make them talk about me. Only it got uncomfortable and gave me a headache. So I did it in the ordinary way," he concluded lamely.

"Well, that was more sensible," said Mrs. Searwood. "But tell me, do you really think you hanged yourself because you'd done so badly with your twenty pounds which had cost another man's life?"

"Yes," replied Old Grady, "that was why I did it, m'lady. Taking another man's life to give me pleasure that turned to dust and never was pleasure at all. Just like Judas."

"Well, I don't think that's why you did it at all," said Mrs. Searwood.

"Begging your pardon, m'lady," said Old Grady with some heat, "but I should know why I committed suicide. It was I who done it. It was my suicide you know."

"I appreciate that," said Mrs. Searwood, "but it isn't that simple. You think you know the reason, but that's because you haven't really thought about it. I'm not blaming you, because lots of people deceive themselves in the same way. But this man that you betrayed—you didn't know him before, did you?"

"No."

"He wasn't a friend of yours and you had no reason to love him or protect him?"

"No."

"In fact, he was your enemy, because he was one of the aristocracy that believed in the divine right of kings. The common people were determined to put an end to that, weren't they?"

"Yes."

"So just because you were the cause of his death was no reason for killing yourself. Since he was really your enemy it was rather a matter for rejoicing, wasn't it?"

"Well," said Old Grady petulantly, "it's been reason enough for me for three hundred years, and I won't be deprived of it. It's a hard thing to have hung myself and then be told that I didn't really have any reason for doing it."

"Oh, I am not denying that you had a reason. It's just that you're befuddled about it, because you haven't allowed yourself to remember the whole story. The parts you don't like about it you've tried to hide, even from yourself, and only told the parts that will arouse sympathy for you. It's disappointing in a way to find spirits using the same tricks as live people. I thought there'd be an improvement."

"Go ahead with your interrogation," said Chief White Feather. "This is getting as good as Socrates."

"Well," said Mrs. Searwood, "I'm only trying to help Old Grady because if you do something like hanging yourself, it's better to know precisely why you did it. Tell me what happened when you found the Cavalier hiding in the hen house."

"I told on him," mumbled Old Grady.

"Did he know you had found him?"

"Yes."

"And you promised that you wouldn't betray him?"

"Yes." The reply was almost inaudible.

"Well, there it is," said Mrs. Searwood. "It's really quite plain. You didn't hang yourself because you had betrayed a man who was really your enemy and probably deserved killing anyway. You hanged yourself because you betrayed a trust. A trust is much more important than one man or even a thousand. Nothing is possible without it. You have to be able to trust people to live, to love them, to help them or have them help you. In betraying your trust you broke with something on which the whole of society is based. The immediate consequence in your case was the death of this man, but that wasn't really important. You'd have shot him if you found him escaping or met him in battle because he was your enemy.

"I think you really knew deep down that since you had broken your word in a matter of life and death you in a way betrayed all humanity. Death would be better because from then on you couldn't trust yourself and you couldn't trust anyone else, and people can't just live like that. Judas felt that way, I'm sure. It wasn't because he betrayed Christ that he hung himself, but because he had betrayed Christ's faith in him. That's why traitors are put to death in every country—not because they betray their country, but because they betray the whole basis of human living."

"I graduated two hundred and seventy-five times from the wrong universities," said Chief White Feather. "Where did you go to school?"

"I didn't go to school," said Mrs. Searwood. "I had a private tutor."

"He must have been a very remarkable man."

"He was," said Mrs. Searwood thoughtfully. "He taught me all the principles of good behavior and then ran off with my mother. Of course he was a Frenchman and wasn't really to be blamed."

Chief White Feather opened his mouth as if to say something and then closed it and shook his head slowly from side to side.

"We haven't finished with Old Grady," said Mrs. Searwood. "I want him to get straightened out so he will stop haunting the house and I can get to sleep at night. Do you understand now why you killed yourself?"

"Yes," said Old Grady, "I do. But I don't feel any better about it. I don't like to think that I can't be trusted. It's a hard thing to go through eternity with. I know I may not be worth a second chance. But I wish I could have one, I really do."

"Now don't you take on," said Mrs. Searwood. "We all make our mistakes, and I'm sure Chief White Feather can work out something for you."

"You don't want me to go away then?"

"Oh no," said Mrs. Searwood. "After all, you've been here much longer than anyone else. And besides, Chief White Feather was saying that he would like some spiritual companionship, and I've no doubt he will be glad of your company."

White Feather gave her a hard look, and then eyed Old Grady. "I don't know that he'll afford much companionship," he said, "but I could probably spend a year or two teaching him to play chess. And as I said before, I think he may come in useful, though I don't know precisely how."

Old Grady bobbed to him. Then he came to the foot of the bed, fumbling awkwardly with his hands.

"Thank you, m'lady," he said, "thank you." He bobbed again twice, gave her a look of humble devotion, and shambled out with Chief White Feather behind him.

"See if you can close the door," said White Feather.

It closed silently without so much as a squeak.

CHAPTER SEVEN

PARSON PENDLEBURY, having ascertained from Mrs. Skipton that Mrs. Searwood would be home and would welcome a visit (he did not like to drop in on people unless sure he was not inconveniencing them) decided to call on her on his way to the church, St. Cedric's, at the top of the village. He was mildly surprised to discover that he was looking forward to meeting her and wondered whether this might be the result of Mrs. Skipton's warm descriptions, completely unsolicited, of the new arrival in Lower Pupton.

He was fifty-eight years of age, a tall spare man whose brown eyes had a chuckle in them and whose erect carriage told of a youth more athletic than clerical. He had indeed been a fair cricketer, playing for Hampshire for several seasons, and now, in his more absent-minded moments, given to cutting an offside break to the boundary with his walking stick. It had been one of his favorite batting strokes—the delayed cut. He would wait until it seemed too late to strike the ball and then, stepping back across the wicket, would flick it hard with his bat, deflecting it from the wicket keepers' hands and sending it through the slips for four. Late Cut Larry Pendlebury they had called him in those days and he had several books of yellowed newspaper clippings to attest to his prowess.

He had never married, preferring his pipes, his cricket trophies and reading the sports news in the *Times* to the company of women whom however he always treated with the gentlest courtesy. And he had entered the church not as a result of some dramatic vocation but because the Bishop, who was a cricketer too, had said that the Church needed men like him. The whole of his life as minister had been spent in Lower Pupton. The babies he had baptized had grown up and sired or mothered other babies, he had seen the older people die off one by one, not tragically but ripe with years and ready for rest, and out of all this had come a profound content.

Birth, life and death he held in equal affection, and he hoped that when his time came he would be buried in the churchyard of St. Cedric's in the soil that he loved and among the people he cherished.

But death was far from his thoughts as he prepared to call on Mrs. Searwood. The pressing problem was whether he should take his car—a two-seater Morris Oxford, vintage 1928—and use up some of his petrol ration. Or whether he would take the pony and trap, which he preferred because it wasn't so noisy. He secretly hoped that he would be able to persuade Mrs. Searwood to come with him to see the church, for it was vital that all visitors attend church and show a decent interest in church affairs. The point was, would she mind riding in a pony and trap? He decided that she wouldn't and told the gardener to get it ready.

Mrs. Searwood was weeding the front flower beds when he arrived, and he thought as he pulled up that he had rarely seen a picture quite so charming. She had on a big straw sun hat and a gay print frock. The gloves on her hands made her appear quite tiny, and she smiled very pleasantly at him as he came through the front gate.

"Mrs. Searwood?" he asked, "I hope I haven't caught you at an inconvenient time. I'm Parson Pendlebury and thought I'd drop by and introduce myself since I understand you've come to stay with us for a while."

"I was just doing a little weeding," Mrs. Searwood replied, "but the sun's getting rather hot. I'm so pleased to see you. Mrs. Skipton said you might call. I understand that we share her in common. Do come inside for a minute." She led the way into the living room.

"It's nice to see the Yews occupied again, and by such a charming resident, if I may say so," the parson said gallantly. "You know the house had been closed down for some years before you came. The family moved away to Scotland. I'm always sorry to see people leave the village, but it was the war. He's engaged in some engineering work for the Admiralty. Taunton was the name."

They chatted for a while about the previous tenants and Mrs. Searwood decided that she liked Parson Pendlebury. He was so erect and manly, and quite handsome. Really didn't look elderly at all if you could ignore his beard. But it was a hard beard to ignore, as big almost as a washing board and vaguely familiar. Mrs. Searwood learned later that it was modeled on the beard of the late Dr. Grace the cricketer, whom Parson Pendlebury ranked close to St. George as one of the sanctified among men.

"I was just on my way to the church," the parson said, "and I wondered whether you would like to come along with me. I'm afraid I've only got a pony and trap, but you can see something of the village, and I think you'll rather like the church. It's very old."

Mrs. Searwood said she would be delighted, got her hat and gloves and the two set off, Parson Pendlebury helping her onto the seat with all the accomplishment of a courtier.

"I hope you'll be able to come to the garden party and bazaar on Saturday," he said. "We're quite busy preparing for it now. It's for the church building fund. And it will be a wonderful opportunity for you to meet your neighbors. There'll be egg-and-spoon races and three-legged races and other things and should be a lot of fun. I have to call on Mrs. Wedge later to see about the prizes. Not really to see about the prizes but to talk her, if I can, into giving a particular prize that I know would be very popular and should help us to raise a great deal of money."

"And what is that?" asked Mrs. Searwood.

"Well," said the parson, "it's an especially handsome handbag of white pigskin she bought several years ago. She never uses it, saving it, as she says, for a special occasion which hasn't arrived to date. All the other women in the village are extremely keen on getting it, but she has turned down all offers. I'm hoping I can persuade her to put it up for the coconut shies. We'd charge a special price for tickets and could raise a great deal of money because I know the competition would be keen among the men. But it's a very tall order, I'm afraid, and I'm not at all sure I shall succeed."

"I'm sure you will," said Mrs. Searwood, "if you go about it in the right way."

St. Cedric's lay a mile up the village street, on the crest of a small hill. Beyond, the village ended and the road straggled through wheat fields and pasture lands, dipping and rising past copse and spinney until it met the Andover turnpike and was swallowed in it. The church could hardly be seen from the road, for it was hidden by a number of yew trees dotting the churchyard. The parson explained that the yews, being evergreens, had been regarded in pagan days as the symbol of everlasting life and so were sacred trees. "The dead were always buried near yews," he said, "to symbolize that they did not really die and the practice has continued up to the present time. It's very pretty here in the winter to see the dark green yews against the snow."

Inside, Mrs. Searwood had a feeling that she had walked from the twentieth century into early Christian times. The light in the tiny church was mellow and wise and touched the wooden pews gently on its way to the stone floor. The floor itself was so worn that there was hardly a foot of it even, and the baptismal font, to the right as she entered, had only blobs of stone on it to indicate the original carving.

"One of the oldest in England," said Parson Pendlebury. "Mr. Wedge tells me the font is probably ninth century; quite certainly tenth. But then the whole church itself is ancient. The hammerlock roof dates from the fourteenth century and the southern transept is almost entirely Saxon. We were offered a small organ by the Bishop, but I was rather afraid that the resonance set up might do some damage. As it is, the building is badly in need of repair, though in a parish as small as this it's rather difficult to raise the money.

"Would you like me to show you around?"

"I'd love it," said Mrs. Searwood. "I feel just as if I were a part of it."

"I'm glad you said that," said the parson. "That's the way I've always felt about this particular church, and indeed, it is so much

a part of all who live in the village that it is impossible for me to think of the one without thinking of the other."

He led her to a large flagstone, in the sanctuary before the altar, upon which were carved the words, still faintly visible, *Guillaume le Soeur.*

"He was the Norman knight who received these lands in a grant from the Conqueror after the Battle of Hastings," explained the parson. "The village takes the latter part of its name from him. I've often wanted to have this area roped off but the villagers won't hear of it. I think they feel that it's their church and they don't want it made into a museum or some kind of place that is too precious for them to mingle with as their own. I rather like them for it. But this is not the oldest grave in the church. There is one still older. I'll have to get candles to show you though."

He went to the altar and took down a candlestick, lighting the candles in it. Then he led Mrs. Searwood over to the south transept. She was disappointed to find that the lancet window which should have illuminated the area was boarded up. Parson Pendlebury led her into the transept and, bending down with the lighted candles, showed her a flagstone on the floor. There were the remains of carving on it, but she could not decipher the words.

"This is the resting place of St. Cedric himself," he said. "The church was raised shortly after his death in the ninth century and the original altar stood here. As you can imagine, it was a very tiny church indeed."

"Is much known about his life?" asked Mrs. Searwood.

"Not a great deal that can be relied upon," said the parson. "Mr. Wedge has been doing some research into the village history. He is our antiquarian, you know, and intends to produce a book about Lower Pupton. He says that Cedric was apparently a former thane or war and court companion of one of the Saxon kings. However, he gave up the life of a warrior at an early age to become a hermit, settling here. As was often the case in those times, quite a school of ecclesiastics gathered around him. When the Danes invaded, he left a hermit's life to help repulse them and is credited with saving the village from their ravages. Several miracles were credited to him after his death and he seems to have become, how I am not quite sure, a patron saint of young lovers. Couples who meet in his church for the first time are supposed to be under his special protection—though I'm afraid that that may well have been a device to get young people to come to church."

"How interesting," said Mrs. Searwood, eyeing the parson, who in the candlelight now looked as noble as a prophet.

"What happened to the window?" she asked.

"Oh I'm afraid it was in very poor shape indeed and we thought it best to board it up. It's a stained-glass window, quite old, the figure representing St. Cedric, of course. I would dearly like to have it repaired. But once again it's a matter of money."

"You know," said Mrs. Searwood, "if you don't mind my saying so, I really can't agree with that."

"With what?" asked the parson, who had been thinking how much younger she looked in the soft light of the candles.

"I can't agree that it's just a matter of money getting St. Cedric's window repaired. I'm sure that the people who put it up originally had no more money than the villagers at the present time. The difference was that they wanted the window and they put it up themselves. That's probably how they built the church too. It very likely didn't cost them much at all except for materials. But they wanted their church and they wanted their window, and so they built them without outside help. And I believe that the villagers could do the same thing today if it were put to them in the right way."

Parson Pendlebury didn't reply and Mrs. Searwood was afraid she had annoyed him. He put the candles back on the altar and they went outside together. In the sunlight, he made a late cut at a Scotch thistle by the side of the graveled path with his stick and said, "You mean that I should ask the villagers to work in their spare time on repairing the window and the church?"

"Certainly," said Mrs. Searwood. "It would be much better that way than if some rich man were to give you the money and a lot of strangers were to do the work. It wouldn't really be the village church then any more. It would half belong to someone else."

"You know," said the parson slowly, "I've been planning to get that window repaired for seven years. We've never seemed to have quite enough money. And then the war. That put a stop to everything."

"But don't you see that the war is just the reason why you should have gone ahead?" said Mrs. Searwood gently. "If you stop a work like that because of the war, it just gives one more victory to the enemy. It brings them nearer to their objective and makes their attack more effective. But if the village were to repair the window during the war, then Lower Pupton would score a triumph of its own over the Nazis. It would be like the way St. Cedric defeated the Danes."

"I hadn't thought about it like that," said the parson. "I believe you're right. We should forget about the money and the war and make a start anyway, with the villagers doing most of the work. I think I'll see Mr. Wedge about it right away. He would be able to direct the work and advise on it better than anybody. Would you like to come along and meet him, and we could perhaps discuss the whole thing now?"

Mrs. Searwood said she'd be delighted and they got into the trap. The parson, buoyed at the thought of getting work started on the window at last, flicked his whip as if in command of a coach-and-four and as they started down the road gave a quick wink in the direction of the church.

It was his own private salute to St. Cedric.

CHAPTER EIGHT

MRS. WEDGE, SOMEWHAT OUT OF BREATH, opened the door for the parson and Mrs. Searwood. She had made a dash to get to the door before either of the twins, who loved to open it themselves and give somewhat surprising and at times uncomplimentary answers to callers.

She was a stout woman with iron-gray hair and was addicted to the wearing of royal-purple frocks and long amber necklaces, which was the combination she had on at the time. Mrs. Wedge was a bubbling woman. She bubbled out of her clothing and she bubbled in her conversation, each word as it were swelling eagerly over the next and each subject breathlessly chasing its predecessor away, so that from the time she opened the door to Mrs. Searwood and the parson to the time she had seated them in her living room she had touched on geraniums, the twins, lawn moth, the garden party, the weather, and no small part of the history of a relative who lived in Australia.

Indeed, it was quite impossible to take the conversation from her, and the parson and Mr. Wedge seemed well accustomed to this. The former balanced a teacup on his knee and nodded gravely in the midst of the verbal torrent, as if he were treading water until there was an opportunity to swim. Mr. Wedge, with a little smile to Mrs. Searwood, seated himself on a pile of logs by the side of the fireplace, ignoring the chairs, and examined the ends of his fingers as if he had just discovered them.

"And how do you like Lower Pupton?" asked Mrs. Wedge and then without waiting for an answer said, "You know the parson is holding a garden party on Saturday for the church building fund— it is for the church isn't it, Mr. Pendlebury?—and I do hope you'll be there. Garden parties are so much fun though I can't stand flies. Still it's early in the year and maybe there won't be so many of them. I think it's the children with that sticky candy. Though they don't seem to mind the flies at all. My husband says there must be some connection between summer flies and polio though we haven't had any in Lower Pupton for three years. Four years ago, one of the village children came down with it and went to the hospital in Winchester. They didn't use an iron lung though. I believe they're rather short of them. They're much too heavy anyway and you'd think they could invent something lighter."

Mrs. Searwood was surprised to discover that in less than a minute the conversation had been veered round from the garden party to a discussion of the weight of iron lungs, and the feat set her mind spinning.

The parson cleared his throat. "It was about the garden party that I really came to see you," he said.

"How nice," said Mrs. Wedge. "I believe they had one over in Littleton the other day and one of the riders—it was a gymkhana really—broke his leg. Or maybe it was a horse."

"My dear," said Mr. Wedge, a thin white wisp of a man in a thin gray wisp of a suit, "I believe Mr. Pendlebury has something to say."

"Oh," said Mrs. Wedge and stopped. She stopped so suddenly, so unexpectedly, that for a second the other three were at a loss. Then the parson leaped into the breach saying quickly, "Yes. You know the proceeds are to go for the repair of the church, and Mrs. Searwood has all but convinced me that we should not wait until the building fund has been completely subscribed. Rather, she says, and I quite agree with her, we should take what money we can raise, and then organize the villagers to do the repairs themselves.

"We have a great deal of skilled labor in the village you know— there's the carpenter, who is really a fine craftsman, and Mr. Budders the stonemason is so excellent an artisan he has been called upon to do work in Winchester many times and there are several others. However (turning to Mr. Wedge), I wanted to get your advice, since you really know far more about the church than anybody else in the village. Do you think it could be done?"

Mr. Wedge, who, perched upon the stack of logs, looked remarkably like a marmoset, pursed his lips in such a way as to convey a whole world of doubt. He cocked his head on one side and eyed the whole room, his eyes finally coming to rest on his wife's enormous amber necklace with its background of royal purple.

"Yes," he said eventually to everyone's surprise. "Yes, I believe it could be done. And I should say for not much more than fifteen hundred pounds. The main damage, of course, is the St. Cedric's window. I understand the stained-glass pieces themselves are intact, but the masonry work needs complete overhauling. We shall have to be absolutely sure to get the correct dimensions of the window frame and the correct proportions too. But I believe I can work it out. I have a scale drawing somewhere which I intend to use as one of the plates in my book. We can work from that and should not have too much trouble."

"Fifteen hundred pounds!" exclaimed the parson, quite crestfallen. "I'm not at all sure that we can raise anywhere near that much. We only have three hundred and eighty pounds in the building fund you know, and although I know that people will be as generous as they can, eleven or twelve hundred pounds is an enormous sum to try to raise in a village of this size."

"There's no need to do all the work at once," replied Mr. Wedge. "The window could be attended to first. I think that might be done for five hundred, or perhaps even less if we all gave our time to it, and I'm sure I shall be only too glad to help."

"That's very very kind of you indeed," said Mr. Pendlebury. "Your services will be invaluable. Now, if we can get together some really good prizes for the games at the garden party we may be able with this one event to raise enough to repair the window.

"I'm hoping we can make at least twenty pounds with the coconut shies. We might charge two shillings a throw and have a grand prize—something really attractive—for whoever makes the best score out of ten tries."

He paused, and Mrs. Wedge, sensing in the silence that followed that her pigskin bag was in danger, surprisingly said not a word. The temptation to seize the conversation by the ears and drag it through an encyclopedia of subjects was almost overwhelming. But the parson had approached her on the subject of the handbag before and she had very nearly weakened, and knew that the future of her prized possession rested in her saying not a word at the present juncture.

Mrs. Searwood came to the rescue. She had been noticing, out of the corner of her eye, the twins playing in the garden. They were playing a favorite game of children from the poorer parts of London—throwing stones at a target which in this instance consisted of the lid of a shoe box propped up against a hedge. And they were remarkably good at it. Although they were standing some distance off, they rarely missed the lid and indeed more often than not hit it dead center.

"I suppose," she inquired innocently, "that one could have a champion, as it were, for the contest. I mean, someone else could throw for us. I'm not at all sure that I could throw very well and most of the ladies would be in the same position."

"Oh certainly," said the parson, "that will be quite understood. In fact, we expect the men and boys to do most of the throwing for the honor of the ladies, rather like in an old-time tournament."

"How nice," said Mrs. Searwood.

"I'd like to look over this scale drawing I have of St. Cedric's window," said Mr. Wedge, rather to the parson's dismay, for it shifted the conversation immediately away from the vital topic of prizes. Mr. Wedge rummaged among the drawers of an expansive desk and came back with a sheaf of papers which he spread on the ground for the parson's inspection. In the meantime Mrs. Searwood whispered something in Mrs. Wedge's ear and the two turned to watch the twins, who by now had cut the lid of the cardboard box almost to ribbons. There was but a sliver of it left, and a stone thrown as swift and straight as a quarrel from a crossbow flicked this to the ground. The twins then without the slightest consultation or hesitation, as if the whole thing had been agreed between them from the time they got up in the morning, commenced to pull each other's hair.

Mrs. Searwood said something more to Mrs. Wedge, who unlocked the floodgates and let a spate of dammed-up verbiage flow out, so fast, so varied, so vigorous and so unconnected that Mrs. Searwood found herself reflecting that enough topics were touched upon to last a normal woman for half a year. At the end of it, however, Mrs. Wedge turned to the parson, now on his hands and knees with Mr. Wedge poring over the drawings of St. Cedric's window, and said, "If it would be of any help at all, I should be very glad to offer my pigskin bag as one of the prizes for the coconut shies. Of course, you have agreed, haven't you, that other people can throw for us in the contest. I got it from Harris's the bootmakers, in the Strand you know. He only makes boots and shoes. But he made the handbag for one of those Indian maharajahs and he hadn't time to pick it up because Gandhi had gone on another fast. I never could understand why it was that that man wouldn't eat. Still, they do say that the less you eat the more brainy you are, except fish of course. Fish are supposed to be very good for the brain though I've known several people who were poisoned by them. Once at Bognor . . ." The flood rolled on and it was several minutes before Parson Pendlebury could find an opportunity to thank Mrs. Wedge for the offer of the handbag and assure her that it would be the most eagerly contested prize in the whole bazaar.

Mrs. Wedge went to fetch it then—a handsome thing so beautifully worked that it was not possible to find a single stitch in the leather. It had some of the placid glow of white jade and the clasp along the top was of ebony, giving it the most aristocratic air, and each tried to outdo the other in admiring it. Mrs. Wedge told the whole story of it once again this time starting with the maharajah and ending up curiously enough with a few rapid comments on fire engines. And then the parson and Mrs. Searwood took their leave.

"You certainly are a remarkable woman," he said admiringly. "Why in one day you've brought almost within my grasp the project for repairing St. Cedric's window, with which I have been concerned for the past several years.

"However did you manage the persuade Mrs. Wedge to offer her handbag?"

"Oh," said Mrs. Searwood, "I told her that she would get it back. A woman you know will risk anything at all provided it is thoroughly understood that she isn't going to lose it."

"Good heavens!" said the parson, "however could you give her such an assurance? We have to be absolutely fair, you know. Everybody has got to have an equal chance. The slightest intimation that there was any—er—er— The slightest suspicion that there was any prior agreement as to who was going to win would be disastrous to all our work."

"Don't worry," said Mrs. Searwood, "everybody will have a fair chance. But there's got to be a winner and it might as well be Mrs. Wedge."

"I'm not at all sure that I follow you," said the parson, seriously disturbed.

"It will be quite fair," said Mrs. Searwood. "The handbag will go to whoever scores highest. Nothing could be fairer than that. Only Mrs. Wedge is going to win and don't worry about it any more."

That night she told Chief White Feather all about the day's adventures and he was very pleased with her.

"That Mrs. Manners," he said, "has been winding up for a broadcast. I dropped in on her and her husband over tea, and she was trying out on him a story that you are the wife of Rudolph Hess."

"Rudolph Hess?" said Mrs. Searwood in astonishment.

"Yes. Rudolph Hess. The right-hand man to Hitler who flew over at the beginning of the war to try to negotiate a settlement and was imprisoned."

"However could she get that idea?"

"Well, it's partially your own fault," said White Feather. "You shouldn't arrive in a small English village in the middle of a war with Germany where there's precious little to talk about with Hotel Adlon, Berlin, labels on your baggage. And your habit of talking to me as if other people could see me also hasn't helped. It's Mrs. Manners's brilliant theory that as Rudolph Hess's wife you came over with him and were imprisoned in the Tower of London. The confinement began to prey on your mind and the situation wasn't helped by the constant questioning of Scotland Yard inspectors. Eventually it was decided that you were quite harmless and the authorities permitted you to come to Lower Pupton to regain your mental balance."

"Why, I've never been in the Tower of London in my life," retorted Mrs. Searwood indignantly.

"And let's hope you never will," said Chief White Feather. "But I'm very pleased to hear that you have made such a good impression on the Wedges and on Parson Pendlebury. They will help to put a stop to Mrs. Manners's speculations."

CHAPTER NINE

CHIEF WHITE FEATHER looked Mrs. Searwood over critically and then gave her a nod of approval.

"My dear," he said, "you look like a duchess. I don't know quite what it is that I like about picture hats, but I've always found them most becoming, and you have just the face and figure for them."

"Go away with you," said Mrs. Searwood, enormously pleased, and then she added, a little sadly, "that's the first compliment I've had in twenty years, and it had to come from a ghost—but at least you're a man."

She had been at great pains to dress herself in her very best for Parson Pendlebury's garden party, and she had to admit that she was both surprised and pleased with the results. The flowered organdy dress she had bought the year before the war in a fit of extravagance was a little short but had been brought into style by letting the hem down. The pattern of lilac blooms was just a little faded—not quite as fresh as she would like for such an important occasion—but nonetheless it was not bad, and the two rips in the back which at first had driven her to despair were nicely mended and really hardly showed at all.

She should have had lilac gloves to match the pattern of her dress and hat, but couldn't find a pair anywhere and had had to content herself with white. But they, thank goodness, were elbow-length and although a little yellowed on the palm and between the fingers, not so badly as to be noticeable. Altogether she felt very well turned out and looked forward to a pleasant and exciting afternoon.

It was the best of garden-party weather. The early May sun was warm but there was still enough breeze to stir the smallest branches of the trees and keep the air gently circulating. From the back of the Yews she could hear doves crooning softly, a peaceable and soothing sound. Indeed, all the world seemed renewed and confident as if after the end of a bitter night, light and growth had at last been restored. It was indeed as if there were no war at all, and to complete her little mirage of peace the parson was sending the pony and trap for her. She had preferred it to his offer of a car, for it reminded her of steadier and more leisurely times.

Everything worked out splendidly. Her worst moment—the descent from the trap before the parsonage—passed without any trouble from an extemporized garter, and Parson Pendlebury was waiting to greet her when she arrived.

"So good of you to come," he said formally, but smiling as to an old friend. "Everybody's very anxious to meet you and hear how things are in London. I'm afraid I shan't be able to get a moment with you." And he permitted himself to give her hand just the suspicion of a squeeze. He looked very handsome indeed in his gray slacks and blue jacket, smoking his pipe, and Mrs. Searwood experienced just the slightest tingle as he took her arm and led her through the cool parsonage, with its Edwardian furnishings, to the garden at the rear. There the lawn was bright with people and parasols. There was a hum of conversation rather like the swarming of bees, with now and then a clear tinkle of laughter. Mrs. Searwood went through a flurry of introductions and *How-do-you-dos* while she eyed every dress in sight and was gratified to see that nobody was wearing anything that wasn't definitely prewar.

This, in its way, was a prewar gathering, though held in the midst of hostilities. The women were dressed in frocks and hats they had bought in the mid- and late thirties—some without even an attempt to accommodate them to present styles. If you looked closely, there was evidence of the neatest mending around hems and necklines. Shoes were a little worn at the heels and frayed across the straps, their buckles not quite as bright as they had once been. And hats had lost some of their sweep and showed a tendency to droop although carried with brave defiance of the times. As Mrs. Searwood circulated among the guests, with a nod here and a pleasantry there, she was conscious of drifting more and more into the past, which she remembered as having been sunny and leisured and confident. It was, she reflected, as if a spell had been cast on the vicar's garden which had moved the calendar back twenty years to the mid-twenties when there had been tennis teas and whist drives and bazaars such as this and vacations by the sea and trips on the Dover boat to the Continent, and even Chief White Feather caught the mood for he said to Mrs. Searwood, "The greatest virtue of you English is your ability to pretend things away."

"It isn't pretense," said Mrs. Searwood, "but practical realism. This *is* peace. All outside the garden may be at war. But this is peace here and we are living in the twenties again."

"I quite agree with you," said a voice behind her and she turned to find Mr. Wedge at her elbow. He had become separated from his wife, who in her royal-purple dress had backed a rather dazed young man in the uniform of the Royal Air Force up against a lemonade cooler and was strafing him with a barrage of chatter.

"Pardon me for interrupting your reverie," Mr. Wedge continued, "but I was just thinking the same thing myself. I was thinking too that although the war has been dragging on now for five years, with the worst probably yet to come, it must finally give way to peace, for war is only temporary and peace the natural condition. Then we will be able to go back to our old ways and I for one will continue my study of the history of Lower Pupton le Soeur."

"Parson Pendlebury tells me you are writing a book about the village," said Mrs. Searwood. "Do tell me something of it."

"Well, it's not a book in the sense of something for general circulation," Mr. Wedge replied. "It's really just a study for myself and a few people who might be interested. Not many, of course, care about the village, so I don't pretend that it will have any popular appeal and I shall have to have it privately printed. Yet the more I delve into the history of Lower Pupton, the more I find it to be almost the story of all people everywhere. It is the way in which it has survived that is so remarkable. It is ancient—as ancient I suspect as the civilized history of the island. There seems to have been a Lower Pupton even before the Norman conquest or the arrival of St. Cedric here. And the village has persisted despite the most formidable odds and vicissitudes. It survived Roman, Dane and even Norman invaders. Only four of the inhabitants, as far as I have been able to establish, outlived the Black Death. Yet they were sufficient to re-establish the village.

"I've readily traced the records back to the Domesday Book. Quite a few of the present families are mentioned by name in the Conqueror's inventory of the lands of his new kingdom. Some, of course, settled here later. The Briggses for instance. That's the boy talking to my wife. They came here about six hundred years ago and were Flemings, though the popular story is that they are of gypsy stock. The Skipton family has lived here for seven hundred years. And my house, you know—the tennis court as it's called. Well, that's what it used to be. It was a tennis court, paved for the game of tennis as it used to be played in the time of Henry V. I've uncovered some of the original paving of the court under the kitchen floor. It was there, I have reason to believe, that the French Dauphin sent the tun of tennis balls that angered Henry into war and led to the conquest of France in the fifteenth century."

"How very interesting," said Mrs. Searwood.

"Your own house, the Yews, has quite an interesting history too," said Mr. Wedge, warming to his subject. "I suppose you've heard some of it already—about the haunting of Old Grady . . ."

"We got him to stop that," said Mrs. Searwood before she could prevent herself.

"You what?" asked Mr. Wedge in surprise.

"Oh, I just don't believe in ghosts," she said nervously and then, anxious to switch the conversation added, "I've heard about the Briggs boy and I would rather like to meet him. I see that he's talking to that rather pretty girl there now. Perhaps we shouldn't intrude."

"Ronnie won't mind," said Mr. Wedge, "provided you let him talk about airplanes. The girl is Christine Adams, from Winchester. Come along and I'll introduce you."

Ronnie Briggs turned out on closer inspection to be a fair-haired young man with the palest blue eyes Mrs. Searwood could ever remember seeing. They were all the more remarkable because they peeped at her from behind an enormous moustache as thick as a hedge and as fierce as a porcupine.

"Pleased to meet you," he said. "This is Miss Adams. Miss Christine Adams."

"How do you do my dear," said Mrs. Searwood. "You look perfectly charming in that lovely blue frock."

"Thank you," said Christine, and smiled. She was a full head and shoulders shorter than her escort, and had a frank and comely look, enhanced by a snub nose and a cap of gold hair bobbed and cut across the front in a neat fringe.

"I understand," said Mrs. Searwood to Ronnie, "that you'll be a pilot soon. It must be very complicated flying those airplanes."

"Got my wings up already," Ronnie replied, nodding slightly towards his chest. "The old man put the promotion through last week. Oh, it's not so hard. Rather fun, really. Actually not much more difficult than learning to ride a bicycle. Something the same in fact. You have to get a feeling of balance and if you don't get it, well, you'll never fly."

He plunged into an increasingly technical discussion of propeller pitch, air speed, angle of approach, dead-stick landings, kinetic force and inertia. Somewhere Mrs. Searwood got the idea that if something in your ears didn't act like a spirit level, you'd fly into a cloud right way up and might come out of it upside down.

"Goodness," she said, "I didn't know that clouds had that kind of effect on airplanes."

She would have broken the conversation off then because the details and technicality were too much for her, but she noticed Mrs. Manners hovering near, and to avoid getting involved with her asked another question.

"What is the easiest kind of airplane to fly?" she said. An enthusiastic flood of technicalities poured from Ronnie until Mrs. Manners had gone and Parson Pendlebury came to the rescue.

"There's just time to show you around the garden," he said, "before the coconut-shies competition opens. We've all got to be in on that, you know," he said meaningly to Ronnie. "There's a wonderful grand prize, a handbag that I'm sure Miss Adams would be very proud to have."

He took Mrs. Searwood's arm and led her away. "I hope you are fond of gardens," he said, "otherwise you'll find this place rather dull. I've put in a lot of time laying it out and chose my flowers more for sentiment than for appearances. Canterbury bells, for instance. Lots of people don't like them, but I put in those beds because they always remind me of Chaucer and somehow he's always seemed more alive to me than many of my contemporaries."

> *"Summer is come in,*
> *Loud sing cuckoo!*
> *Groweth seed and bloweth mead*
> *And springeth the wood new—"*

quoted Mrs. Searwood, and was rather surprised that she remembered the extract, for she had learned it as a girl, though vague about the author.

The parson beamed. "Bless my soul," he said, "I don't think I've heard that for thirty years."

"Don't ask me for the rest of it," said Mrs. Searwood. "I'm sure I've forgotten."

"Let me see," mused the parson, stroking his beard and contemplating the Canterbury bells. "Ah yes:

> *"Ewe bleateth after lamb,*
> *Cow* (I think) *after calf cu.*
> *Bullock starteth, buck verteth,*
> *Merrie sing cuckoo."*

They laughed together. "I don't suppose many people bother to read that kind of thing these days," Mr. Pendlebury said. "There are so many other demands on the attention of young folk now. I was quite a reader when I was younger and I think got more lasting pleasure out of reading than is perhaps obtained from going to the movies or listening to the wireless."

Mrs. Searwood nodded: "The quality of pleasure has changed," she said. "There doesn't seem to be much that is restful in amusement these days—it's all exciting and energetic. I'm afraid I can't keep up with it. Serenity and quiet have gone—they're fugitives I suppose from a more vigorous generation. And yet we were vigorous in our day. I used to go bicycling thirty or forty miles in a day sometimes. We had great fun, singing all the old songs like 'Lily of Laguana' and 'Bicycle Built for Two.'

"But when I came into your garden here and saw all the people brightly dressed and chatting together I felt as if I were back in saner times. It is nice, isn't it, to be able to worry again for a while about not dripping tea on a frock or treading on the hem of your dress when you stand up. Though you wouldn't know about such things, being a man."

"No," said the parson, "but I understand what you mean. Still, when it's all over, things will return to normal again."

"I wonder," said Mrs. Searwood. "I wish they would, but I don't really think they will. They'll be different because everything has to change. There is no such thing as remaining still, and I get a feeling sometimes that I'm tiring myself out trying to keep pace."

"You shouldn't try to keep pace," Mr. Pendlebury said gravely. "Our time was thirty years ago, and that is the time we should continue to try to live in. Let the younger people go on to the newer things they seek. It's natural that they should. But I think the wisest thing for people of our generation is to stay in our own times. We're comfortable in them, and if others say we're old-fashioned, that is no disgrace."

"Perhaps you're right," replied Mrs. Searwood. "It's really no use struggling against being old when you are old."

"My dear Mrs. Searwood," said the parson, "if you are old then you lend to that condition all the charm of youth."

Mrs. Searwood blushed. "Thank you," she said, "that's the second nice thing someone's said about me today."

He bowed. "Come. Let me show you the rest of the garden," he said, "before the sports program starts."

He gave her his arm with the grace of a courtier and led her over to the rose garden through a trim hedge of privet. His step was perhaps a little more sprightly than natural to his years and Chief White Feather, noting this, said to himself:

> *"Love hath a magic over life*
> *That makes the autumn leaf*
> *a fruit of gold."*

He couldn't decide whether the quotation was original with himself or from his friend Kit Marlowe, and this annoyed him.

CHAPTER TEN

RONNIE BRIGGS HAD BEEN GOING what was for him steady with Christine for the past three months. Not that he was of a flirtatious disposition, but up to then girls had meant rather less than spark plugs to him, and he had become accustomed to think of them as a somewhat lesser kind of human being, always tagging around on the fringes of a male circle and something of a minor nuisance.

He had gone to a dance at Winchester three months before and had met Christine and been unhappy ever since. She bothered him. When he was with her he didn't know quite what to talk about except airplanes, of which she knew nothing. And when he was away from her, he found himself talking to her about all manner of subjects none of which included airplanes.

Corky Peters from Andover had explained what was the matter. "You've had it, old man," he said. "You're in love. There's only one way to cure it. Stay away for a month. Take my advice. I know. I fall in love three times a year of an average, and when I see the church door looming, I stay away and I'm a free man again." So Ronnie had stayed away for a month and had never been so miserable in all his life. In the end he'd hopped on his motor bike and gone over to Winchester to ask Christine to the garden party.

All the way over he chided himself for listening to Corky, and then grew quite panicky at the thought that Christine might have moved, or might be going with someone else or might refuse to see him.

So it was a great relief when he arrived to find her safe, and unattached, and delighted at the prospect of going to the garden party with him.

The trouble now was that things hadn't gone so well. He hadn't been able to get a moment alone with her. First Mrs. Wedge had cornered him and he'd thought he'd suffocate before she got through. Then Mr. Wedge had brought over the lady from London and he'd had to talk to her about airplanes (though he liked talking about airplanes). And then Admiral Gudgeon had come along to give him a lecture on the inferior role of the Air Force compared with that of the Navy, without which, he said, there never would have been an England in the first place. And then Mrs. Manners had come along to ask whether Rudolph Hess had a wife, as if he knew, and had hinted that he had and furthermore that Mrs. Hess was quite close by.

"Come along," he said to Christine at last, "let's go somewhere quiet where we can have a chance to talk."

They found a bench at the southern end of the rose garden, sheltered by an arbor of ramblers, and sat down on it. Once they had sat down, Ronnie wished miserably that he had given more attention to girls and what to say to them. There must be some way, he knew, of saying what he felt, or leading up to it at least, without feeling as awkward as a cow that has stepped in a milk bucket. He cleared his throat, straightened the edge of his moustache with his fingers and said:

"Nice day."

"Gorgeous," said Christine.

Her voice had a delicious little thrill of mirth to it, and her hair caught the sun almost like a halo. She was absolutely wizard, a real smasher, and he felt all the more miserable realizing that now he had met this terrific girl he couldn't say what he wanted to her.

Christine got up from the bench, as graceful as a princess, and picked a partially opened white rose from a bed near by. "The roses will be out soon," she said. "I've always liked roses."

It was quite an ordinary thing to say, and yet to Ronnie it sounded like the most wonderful sentence that had been uttered in the whole history of human conversation.

"Rather," he said quickly, anxious to seize the coattails of what he hoped would be some kind of useful discussion. "I like roses too."

"You like flying better, don't you?"

"Well—er— Well, they're different. A chap can't concentrate on roses unless he's a poet or something. I'm not a poet."

"I know," said Christine, "you like flying. And I'm glad of it. I'm glad you got your wings. I was worried about you. I thought you'd flunked out and that was why you hadn't come to see me. Sometimes I thought that you'd had an accident. You shouldn't worry people like that."

"Were you really worried about me?" asked Ronnie breathlessly.

"Of course I was," replied Christine. "Why did you stay away? It was pretty beastly of you, you know. You were always calling on me for two months, and then you stopped all of a sudden. Why did you do that? I think you owe me an explanation."

"Well, I wanted to be sure."

"Sure about what?"

Ronnie swallowed hard. He put his hands in his lap and stared straight ahead at a rosebush as if it were his wing commander. "I wanted to be sure about the way I felt," he said.

"What way do you feel?"

This is it, thought Ronnie. This is like the first solo landing flying blind. In just a second you'll be down safe or you'll be washed out. He took a deep breath, and then suddenly in the silence there was a loud, high-pitched scream from the hedge behind. He jumped up and peered over the hedge, Christine following more slowly.

At the foot of a crab-apple tree, one of the Wedge twins was squirming on the ground holding onto his wrist. His brother standing beside him was hollering at the top of his voice. Tears streamed down both their faces.

"What's the matter?" demanded Ronnie, pushing through the hedge.

"Bert fell out of the tree and broke his arm," said the twin who was standing up. Ronnie picked the boy up and examined his arm while the two of them howled their misery.

"It's all right," he said. "It isn't broken. It's just bruised. That's all." By this time a little crowd had gathered, with Mrs. Wedge in the forefront.

"Whatever is the matter, Bert?" she said, smothering him in ample folds of purple.

"He's broke his arm, that's what," said the other twin. And he added, "And I've broke mine too." Ronnie explained that the boy had apparently fallen out of the tree but that the arm was only bruised.

"Oh," exclaimed Mrs. Wedge in sudden dismay, "my handbag. And the coconut shies just going to start. But you'll be able to throw for me, won't you Fred. You're just as good at throwing as Bert, aren't you?"

"No, I won't," said Fred. "My arm hurts too. If his arm hurts, then my arm hurts. In the same place."

"Come, come," said Mrs. Wedge very perturbed, "you didn't fall from the tree. It can't possibly hurt you."

"It does too," said Fred, stubbornly, "same place as his'n."

"But you must throw for me to win back my handbag," Mrs. Wedge wailed.

"I can't throw," said Fred adamantly, "and neither can he. We've both broken our arm."

"You've got to do something about the coconut shies," Mrs. Searwood said to Chief White Feather. "The twins have hurt themselves—at least one of them has and the other thinks he has—and somebody's going to win Mrs. Wedge's handbag."

"That's what she put it up for as a prize, isn't it?" asked White Feather.

"Don't be silly. You don't think she'd put it up as a prize if she wasn't sure she'd win it back herself? The twins were going to throw for her and they're easily the best shots in the whole village. I watched them and I know. But now what's to be done? Mrs. Wedge certainly can't throw, and I doubt Mr. Wedge can either. And if she loses her handbag, she won't talk to me for weeks."

"Well, what do you expect me to do?"

"Well, you've got all those degrees, you should be able to think of something."

"I'm not sure that I agree with your line of thought at all," said Chief White Feather. "It doesn't seem sporting to me. Mrs. Wedge offers the prize, but only so that she can get it back. And then you want me to fix it so that she does get it back. What about all the other people? They're supposed to have an equal chance you know."

"You men are all the same," said Mrs. Searwood. "Parson Pendlebury was talking just like that. You boggle over some silly little principle forgetting that it isn't the handbag at all that matters but St. Cedric's window. I persuaded Mrs. Wedge to put the handbag up so that we could raise money for the window but on the distinct understanding that she got the bag back again. It's far more important that we get the window repaired than that somebody else gets the handbag. If it's unsporting to help repair a beautiful stained-glass window then I'm unsporting."

"Well," said Chief White Feather, "I'll see what I can do. But I'm still not sure that I like it."

They moved off to where a huge crowd was gathered around the coconut shies. Parson Pendlebury was standing on a chair, exhibiting Mrs. Wedge's beautiful handbag and explaining the rules of the contest, and Mrs. Wedge was surreptitiously shaking the uninjured twin in an effort to pressure him into throwing for her.

"Two shillings a throw," said the parson, "with the prize going to the best out of ten. But we must have at least ten contestants. All the money is to go to the repair of St. Cedric's window and we hope to arrange for a volunteer force of helpers from the village to put the work in hand immediately. This handmade pigskin bag is the work of one of the finest craftsmen in London and I'm assured that it is the only one of its kind anywhere and could not be purchased for under fifty pounds. I'm sure that the men in the audience will be very anxious to secure such a prize for their ladies. I'll keep score myself, and the bag will be handed over immediately to the winner."

Mrs. Wedge uttered a moan of real pain.

"Now," continued the parson, "who will be the first to buy tickets?"

Ronnie Briggs was already at the ticket booth, closely followed by a perturbed Mr. Wedge, who was so nervous that he lost his tickets as soon as he had bought them and created quite a commotion until he found them in his breast pocket. Then came Green the carpenter, then Budders the stonemason. Five others followed in quick succession, then two or three more. Parson Pendlebury requested and received permission by voice vote from the crowd to try himself and was surprised to find Mrs. Searwood standing at the booth with her tickets in her hand.

"My dear Mrs. Searwood," he said, "this really isn't necessary. You've already done so much to inspire this work and help it on its way that I don't feel you have to subscribe from your own pocket."

"But I've got to get that handbag back for Mrs. Wedge," replied Mrs. Searwood, and the parson gave her a look of pure amazement.

Budders was the first to try his hand. The name coconut shy was more traditional than descriptive of the contest. Ten groups of three wooden bottles, weighted in the base, had been set up on stands with a cloth backdrop behind them. The object was to knock over as many of the wooden bottles as possible with ten balls. Budders scored eight with his first three balls, missed completely with the next two; took careful aim with the sixth and knocked over one bottle, missed again with the seventh and eighth, lost his temper with the ninth and tenth and ended up with a total score of thirteen out of a possible thirty.

Green, who came next, did better with seventeen. Mr. Wedge, who couldn't stand the strain any longer, managed a truly heroic nine and so it went on, with Ronnie Briggs and the parson tied at twenty-four.

"It looks as though we shall have to have a runoff," said the parson. "I'm delighted to see that I haven't lost my old cricketing ability."

"I think Mrs. Searwood's next," said Ronnie, weighing one of the wooden balls in his hand while Christine stood beside him, glowing with pride.

"Of course," said Mr. Pendlebury. "This way, Mrs. Searwood."

"Drat that Indian," said Mrs. Searwood, looking anxiously around for Chief White Feather. "I wonder where he could have gone to?" He was nowhere in sight.

"Were you looking for someone?" asked the parson.

"Not exactly," replied Mrs. Searwood. "Oh dear. I do hope I can throw straight." She glanced at Mrs. Wedge, who was looking pure venom at her.

"May I throw underhand?" she asked the parson.

"Any way you wish," he replied gallantly.

Mrs. Searwood put one leg determinedly before her, shut her eyes and threw the ball. It plopped miserably on the grass in front of her without even reaching the stands where the wooden bottles stood.

"You'll have to do better than that," said Chief White Feather, popping up from behind the stands.

"I'm doing my best," said Mrs. Searwood.

"I know you are," said the parson, "and it's very sporting of you to try at all."

"Throw them to me," said Chief White Feather, "and I'll attend to the rest." To the audience, it seemed that the next ball described a soft and quite useless parabola until it got near the bottles when it suddenly darted off and knocked over six of them.

There was a gasp of astonishment and Chief White Feather called out, "For goodness' sake, get them a little nearer. I can't produce miracles, you know."

"I'm trying as hard as I can," said Mrs. Searwood, and the parson looked at her in pure astonishment. "A break from the off in mid-air," he exclaimed. "I've never seen it done before."

The third ball was a fair throw and knocked over three bottles on its own though it seemed to Mr. Pendlebury, who was watching it closely, that it suddenly dipped when almost on top of them. Numbers four and five were the most astonishing though. The fourth hit the top of the back cloth and was falling to the ground when it suddenly reversed itself, sped for the racks of bottles and sent three of them flying. The fifth hit the ground before the stand, suddenly rocketed upward and scattered three more. After that the

balls seemed to take license of all the laws of trajectory and gravity, bounding around and scattering bottles right and left before
the astonished eyes of the gallery, until Mrs. Searwood had
achieved top score of twenty-seven.

"Upon my soul," exclaimed the parson, "I've never seen such
an exhibition. You must have the most remarkable natural talent
for putting a bias on a ball. I can't think of a similar case though
I've seen some first-rate googly bowlers in my time. Wherever did
you get such an ability?"

"I'm sure I don't know," said Mrs. Searwood. "It just happened
that way."

"Well, if I hadn't seen it myself, I never would have believed
it," said the parson. "The prize, of course, is yours, but I wonder
whether you would give me a little demonstration later with a
cricket ball? I'd rather like to see whether I can learn anything from
watching you."

Mrs. Searwood said she really didn't think she could do it ever
again, and the parson, intending to return to the matter later, presented her with the handbag before a crowd silent with awe. Mrs.
Searwood was conscious that although only a few short days in the
village, she had become the most outstanding person there, and
she wasn't at all happy about it.

She took the bag immediately to Mrs. Wedge and returned it to
her. Mrs. Wedge took it from her in a half-frightened way, as if she
didn't really want it any longer.

CHAPTER ELEVEN

MRS. MANNERS WAS ALL THE MORE DETERMINED to find out something further about Mrs. Searwood after her remarkable throwing demonstration at the parson's bazaar. The bazaar had proved successful beyond all expectations. A total of one hundred and twenty pounds had been raised from the various events. A village committee of workers had been organized for the repair of St. Cedric's window and Mrs. Manners had managed to get herself closely associated with the work. This gave her an opportunity for frequent meetings with Mrs. Searwood, but beyond discovering that Mrs. Searwood had a habit of talking out loud to herself and regarded Hitler as her personal enemy, she hadn't been able to turn up much.

The feud between Mrs. Searwood and Hitler, however, gave strength to her theory that the former was the wife of Rudolph Hess. She could understand Hitler being angry with Hess and his anger extending to Hess's wife whom it would obviously be in his interests to destroy. But she wanted to get more details and decided to use Old Grady as a lure for having a good heart-to-heart talk with Mrs. Searwood in her home.

"You haven't seen *him* walking up the stairs at nighttime, have you dear?" she would ask whenever they met. Mrs. Searwood, who now knew that *him* meant Old Grady, was able to reply truthfully that she hadn't.

After a number of inquiries about Old Grady, Mrs. Manners let it be known that she was what was called a spiritualist (she whispered the information so confidentially that she might have been confessing to being a secret nudist). And she added that she was also a medium.

"I hear voices," she said one day, wrapping up a loaf. "Human voices only they don't come from humans. They come from spirits. It's what they call clairaudience. I've studied a good deal about spiritualism and I believe that if we held a séance at the Yews we could find out where Old Grady is."

"But I don't care where Old Grady is," said Mrs. Searwood, stifling an impulse to say that Chief White Feather was teaching him to play chess. "I'm really not much interested in spirits."

"Ah. But the spirits are interested in you," said Mrs. Manners and this startled Mrs. Searwood so much that she nearly dropped the loaf.

"What do you mean?" she asked quickly.

"They cluster around you all the time," said Mrs. Manners.

"Have you seen any?" asked Mrs. Searwood nervously, afraid that Chief White Feather might have become visible to someone else. He himself had told her that in certain mental conditions spirits were readily visible to many people.

"No," replied Mrs. Manners lamely, "as a matter of fact, I've never seen a spirit. But it's my belief that you have a poltergeist—one of those mischievous spirits that play tricks on people. I shall never forget the way those balls acted when you were throwing them at the bazaar. That's a poltergeist if ever there was one. And although I've never actually seen a spirit, I can hear their voices and ask them questions. Maybe there's someone you would like to contact in the beyond. If we had a séance, I could try for you. And I could also get rid of the poltergeist which may one day do you a great deal of harm."

Mrs. Searwood said that she did not have a poltergeist and that there was no one in the beyond with whom she wanted to get in touch. But Mrs. Manners returned to the topic again and again and at last Mrs. Searwood agreed to hold a séance at the Yews as much to get rid of her as anything else.

"You shouldn't have done it," said Chief White Feather, quite angrily, when she told him. "That woman's a mischief-maker and the less you have to do with her, the better off you'll be. Calling me a poltergeist! Why that's the equivalent of calling the Prime Minister a circus clown. Poltergeists are little more than half-wits, completely without education or breeding of any kind. One just doesn't associate with them." He was very upset indeed, and Mrs. Searwood discovered that Chief White Feather was very sensitive on anything touching his dignity and his learning. She said she was sorry but that there had been no way out of it, but White Feather was not mollified.

"For all I know that Manners woman may be a medium with an output like Battersea Power Station," he said, still very angry. "You people don't understand what you're doing when you try to get in touch with the spirit world. You think that spirits are automatically good, though they may have been cutthroats and child stranglers during their human existence. Death doesn't change character you know. Evil people remain evil as spirits. How would you like to have that old lecher Caligula prowling around your drawing room?"

"I wouldn't be worried at all," said Mrs. Searwood, miffed. "I don't believe that evil people can do any harm to good people, or evil spirits either."

"That's fine if you're one hundred per cent good," said Chief White Feather. "The trouble is that no one is. There's bad in everybody. And it is on this that the malevolent spirits batten themselves and plant ideas in people's minds to do things they would never dream of if they hadn't got in touch with the spirit world. The contest between good and evil continues in our world, you know, as strongly as it does in yours. And Caligula has been especially active recently because of the opportunities presented by the war."

"You're talking just like one of those monks in the Dark Ages," said Mrs. Searwood. "I think you must be a little liverish."

"I haven't got a liver," retorted White Feather. "At least, I have a liver only in the spiritual sense, and it doesn't make me liverish, as you call it."

He went away in a sulk leaving Mrs. Searwood to make the preparations for the séance. Mrs. Manners had told her that the room must be dark, and she was glad to see that there were good blackout curtains with which this might be accomplished.

She assumed that she should serve tea, for Mrs. Searwood was devoted to tea and had confessed to Parson Pendlebury that she would attend church more regularly if only tea were served during the sermon. A table, she knew, would be necessary because she had heard that at séances tables rose in the air. The only one in the living room was a mahogany mammoth of the late nineteenth century, and she wanted to ask Chief White Feather whether this would be too heavy for a spirit to lift.

"No, it won't," he said. "And that for the reason that spirits do not lift tables. They are lifted by the mediums, and the heavier you make it the better I'll like it, for I have no use for mediums."

"I don't know what's got into you lately," Mrs. Searwood complained. "You've been mooning around the house like a ghost. Not yourself at all. Is it something I've done? You're not still annoyed about that silly coconut-shy business, I hope. It all helped the work on St. Cedric's and you yourself have admitted it's coming along beautifully."

"No," said Chief White Feather, "it's not that. It's just that I've got a feeling that something's going to happen and I can't quite put my finger on it. There's something bad brewing but I don't know what. I have a sense of danger pending. I just don't know what it is. And I don't like this séance business at all."

"It's just that man Hitler," said Mrs. Searwood with conviction. "He's left me alone too long and I know his spies must have told him that I've moved from London and he is going to bomb me down here. I've been expecting it because of what I said about the Germans when I was in Berlin. Oh dear, I do hope they don't hurt that window after all our trouble. Maybe I ought to tell the parson."

"Nonsense," said Chief White Feather impatiently, "Hitler wouldn't know you if he met you in the family bar of the Fox and Hounds. I can't explain this feeling to you in human terms because it concerns one of the senses of spirits that human beings just haven't got. The nearest that mortals feel that I can compare it to is a sense of foreboding like waiting in a dentist's office. It's a hunch; a prescience that some dreadful event is impending. And it does somehow seem to center around you. If I could contact some other spirit of intellect—Old Grady isn't sensitive to anything but draughts, his chess is atrocious—I might be able to find out what this thing is. But they've all left England, as I told you."

"Then why don't you stay around during the séance?" said Mrs. Searwood practically. "Mrs. Manners might be able to contact someone for you."

"Mrs. Manners," said Chief White Feather contemptuously.

"Only a little while ago you were warning me that she might be as powerful as Battersea Power Station," chided Mrs. Searwood.

"Oh, all right. I'll stay," said White Feather. "It can't do any harm and it will be a relief from Old Grady. That dunderhead says he can't learn chess because he can only think like a pawn since he's never been a knight. Maybe he's right too. He's been a pawn all his years."

"Good," said Mrs. Searwood, relieved. "I really hoped that you would stay because it will help me with Mrs. Manners who is always asking questions. Besides, I always feel more comfortable when you're around. Perhaps you can help with serving tea. Oh no. You'd better not because it might frighten people. I keep forgetting that you're a spirit. Just stay by me and don't let that Caligula lay a hand on me if he turns up. Nasty man. Who was he anyway?"

"A Roman emperor of the time of Christ who delighted amongst other things in drowning young maidens. He made his horse a proconsul, if I remember rightly. He was mad, but mad in a very evil way."

"Well, if he comes, you let me know and I'll let up the window shades and frighten him away," said Mrs. Searwood.

Mrs. Manners, with Mrs. Skipton and Mrs. Wedge, who had also been invited to attend, arrived after dinner. It was still daylight, but the sky was clouded over and little bursts of hot wind swept the street, rustling the bushes and stirring small eddies of dust off the road.

A dog over at the tennis court barked with a touch of hysteria and was answered by another and for a minute there was a clamor of barking which died out just as quickly as it had arisen. The barking made Chief White Feather all the more nervous and he asked Mrs. Searwood whether she couldn't find some excuse for calling the whole séance off. "You'll be sorry if you don't," he warned. But she tut-tutted him down. A window at the top of the house rattled and a door flew open in an upstairs room with such violence that it knocked a picture off a wall.

"It's going to be a terrible night," said Mrs. Manners.

They seated themselves around the mahogany table, with the curtains drawn and the room rescued from the blackness only by a candle which flickered in the center of the table. This threw gargoyle shadows of the women on the walls and ceiling, and Chief White Feather sitting in a corner said the whole thing gave him the creeps.

"Tell her to get on with it," he said impatiently. "This whole place is full of something or other that I don't like and the feeling I've got is getting worse."

Mrs. Manners, considerably impeded by the conversational *non sequiturs* of Mrs. Wedge who had started with palmistry and arrived at the Egyptian pyramids, gave her instructions in a whisper as if she were afraid the spirits she was going to call upon might overhear her, think the whole thing a trick, and refuse to have any part in it.

"Everybody put their hands on the table and stretch them out, thumbs against each other and little fingers touching those of the person next to you. That establishes a kind of field like an electric thing and makes it easier for the spirits to contact us," she said.

Chief White Feather strolled over to take a look. He stood opposite Mrs. Searwood behind Mrs. Manners and watched the proceedings with a kind of contemptuous interest. "Two hundred years ago you'd have had to catch a couple of lizards, boil them and eat their livers," he said. "You're getting off pretty easy."

"Stop being disgusting," said Mrs. Searwood.

Mrs. Manners bridled. "Really, Mrs. Searwood," she said, "I don't see anything disgusting about it. You must have a little more reverence. Criticism or mockery drives the spirits away. Two hundred years ago you'd have had to catch a couple of lizards, boil them and eat their livers."

"Good Lord," exclaimed Chief White Feather, "this woman *is* a medium. She's going into a trance."

It was true. Mrs. Manners stiffened slowly in her chair and raised her little sparrow head. Her eyes were open but staring at a point which seemed to be beyond the wall opposite her.

"Oh dear," said Mrs. Wedge, at a loss for words for the first time that evening, "whatever shall we do?"

"I suppose we'd better ask her some questions," said Mrs. Searwood, "only I don't know of anything I want to ask."

"You're a widow," said Mrs. Skipton, who had always been curious about Mrs. Searwood's deceased husband, "why don't you ask if your husband is happy?"

"I know perfectly well he's happy," said Mrs. Searwood, "because he wouldn't put up with anything else. He always made such a row if anything annoyed him. But I'll ask anyway. I do hope he won't be angry. This is Mrs. Searwood speaking," she continued more loudly. "Is my husband happy?"

"Yes," said Mrs. Manners in a hollow voice.

It wasn't much of an answer. Mrs. Searwood felt cheated that there weren't any more details.

"What's he doing?" she asked.

"I can't understand," said Mrs. Manners. "It's something to do with wheat, but I can't make it out."

"Oh I know," said Mrs. Searwood brightly, "he's still at the same old problem—trying to produce a strain of wheat that will give more yield to the acre. Well, it's nice to know that he's got something to keep him busy through eternity."

"He says it will *not* keep him busy through eternity," said Mrs. Manners. "He seems angry."

"That's my husband, all right," commented Mrs. Searwood. "He never would admit that he'd bitten off more than he could chew."

"Stop asking silly questions," said Chief White Feather sharply. "Ask what is this thing that is going to happen."

"Stop asking silly questions," parroted Mrs. Manners. "Ask what is this thing that is going to happen."

Chief White Feather glared down at her.

"Little Sir Echo."

"Little Sir Echo," repeated Mrs. Manners faithfully.

Mrs. Wedge looked frightened. "I don't like this," she said. "She's talking just as if she was repeating what someone else was saying to her. Like a Gramophone record. I never did trust them. It makes me feel that we're being watched all the time. I really don't like it."

"Well, we'll ask one more question," said Mrs. Searwood, "then we'll turn on the lights and have a nice cup of tea."

"Ask," commanded Chief White Feather impatiently. "Ask."

"Ask," echoed Mrs. Manners.

"What is this thing that is going to happen?" asked Mrs. Searwood.

Mrs. Manners made no sound. She continued to look at the point beyond the wall. But the expression on her face had changed. Her mouth twisted and her eyes widened as if at the sight of some approaching terror.

"No," she whispered. "No."

There was an overpowering smell in the room—a smell of mixed sweat and straw. It seemed to come from beyond the windows. As it increased in strength the expression on Mrs. Manners's face changed to one of panic, and she seemed to be struggling to get up and run away but was restrained by the touching fingers on the table. Little beads of perspiration appeared on her forehead, visible even in the candlelight. Her lips trembled and twitched and out of them, curiously distorted, came the words:

"What is the thing that is going to happen?"

The stench of the stable from behind the curtain was now almost unbearable. Mrs. Wedge let out a little whimper of fright. Mrs. Manners was trying to say something. The words came out of her as from a robot—without expression or inflection.

"*Luna obscurata*," she said, "*hora periculosa*."

"I don't understand a word of it," said Mrs. Searwood.

"Open the curtains!" cried Chief White Feather. "Open the curtains if you value your sanity."

Mrs. Searwood dashed from the table, threw aside the heavy curtains and flung the French windows open. There was a peal of maniac laughter from outside and the neighing of a horse. The sweet night air poured into the room like balm, dispersing the strong stable smell.

"Who was it?" Mrs. Searwood asked trembling. She was very disturbed.

"Talk of the devil," said Chief White Feather.

"That was Caligula. Look. You haven't much time. I know what it is now that's been troubling me. Don't ask any questions. Get these women down to the cellar. Tell them anything you want but get them down there. Right now. Tell them they're going to be bombed."

Mrs. Searwood did so, and everybody was so disturbed by the experience at the séance that they didn't even stop to ask her how she knew. She bundled them all down into the cellar, with blankets and candles, and told them to stay there and she'd be back in a minute. Once she'd closed the door on them she said to Chief White Feather, "Now, what is all this? What were those funny words that Mrs. Manners said?"

"They were Latin and what they meant was, 'When the moon is covered over, is the hour of danger.'"

"Stuff and nonsense," said Mrs. Searwood, but she was shaken anyway.

"Come here," said Chief White Feather and led her to the window. Outside, on the northern horizon, a serene moon shimmered in a sky of black velvet. "Look over to the west," he said. Mrs. Searwood looked and saw a bank of cloud, so solid that it resembled the battlements of a castle. There was not even a smear of light in its density. The moon seemed to be sailing towards it. Soon it would be swallowed in the blackness.

"'When the moon is covered up, is the hour of danger,'" quoted White Feather. "Now get down to the cellar, and have everybody lean with their backs to the walls."

Mrs. Searwood went.

THE MAN IN THE TRENCH COAT looked at the rocket shimmering in the moonlight and felt the blood pound in his throat. "Are you sure it will work?" he asked. He spoke in German, with a slight Austrian accent.

"Certainly, Leader," said the scientist. "It will reach a speed of twelve hundred miles an hour. It will be there in a few seconds. The most exact calculations have been made. When the two hands on the dial coincide, press the button and it cannot fail to strike the center of London. But be sure to fire when the hands come together. A moment's delay will affect the accuracy."

On the big dial, a red hand inexorably chased a small black one. But the man in the trench coat was not watching them. His eyes shifted from the slim pencil of the rocket a hundred yards away to the sky. He noticed that the moon would soon be obscured behind a dense mass of cloud. The contrast between the light of the moon and the darkness of the cloud fascinated him.

"The moon is like life and the cloud is like death," he said aloud. "I will fire when the death of the cloud devours the life of the moon. My intuition tells me that that will be the right moment."

"Leader," pleaded the scientist, "it is not a matter of intuition but of mathematics. We have estimated the precise air temperature at the time of firing, the density and humidity, the speed of rotation of the earth. All are exactly worked out. Ten years' work, my Leader . . . ten years' work. It must be fired at the precise time or all is wasted."

"Mere mathematics," replied the other. "I rely as in all things upon my intuition."

The red hand on the big dial caught up with the black one and passed it, but the rocket remained earth-bound. The scientist groaned. The man in the trench coat remained as one transfixed, his face turned to the sky. The moon commenced to slip behind the cloud bank and the light was drained from the land. When the last sliver of light died, he pressed the button. The rocket shook on its scaffolding, strained almost imperceptibly upward, hovered for a second and then was gone, so swiftly that it was almost impossible to credit that it had ever been there.

"Ruined!" cried the scientist. "Ten years' work all ruined." He could hardly contain his anger. "Do you know where that rocket is going to land now, my intuitive Leader who has no use for mathematics? It will land, according to my calculations, in a remote English village called Lower Pupton le Soeur."

The man in the trench coat shrugged his shoulders, completely unperturbed.

"So?" he said. "Then it is in this little village of Lower Pupton le Soeur that my worst enemy is hiding."

CHAPTER TWELVE

THE FIRST THOUGHT was that it was a volcano—that the earth had opened up and a blast of flame issued from the inner depths and completely destroyed the Fox and Hounds; foundations, walls, roof, furnishings, cellar—everything. Everything that is except Josiah Tanner, proprietor, and one corner of his signboard containing the scarred but undaunted words *Beers and Stouts*.

The volcano theory was never completely shaken, for it fitted in with some of the peculiarities of this phenomenal explosion in the dead of night in the very heart of Lower Pupton le Soeur. For one thing, there had been no plane overhead, so it couldn't possibly have been a bomb—Ronnie Briggs affirmed that no enemy bombers had been nearer than eighty miles of Lower Pupton that night.

Then the crater left by the explosion was huge and bore some of the earmarks of a volcanic cone. Those who entered it before the military police arrived and screened the whole place off said that there was stuff lying around like lava, though when pressed they admitted they had never seen any lava. Still a man could be credited with knowing lava when he saw it. Then there had been the rather odd weather of the night before—hot and puffy with quick little showers of warm rain. Everybody agreed that it was earthquake weather.

That there had never been a volcanic eruption in England in the written history of its inhabitants did not disturb those in Lower Pupton who inclined to the volcano theory. There is always a first time, they said sagely, wagging their heads. There was a lot of talk of moving out before there was a second eruption, but nobody was sure where to move to. And in the end they all decided to stay.

Another theory was that enemy agents had planted a time bomb under the Fox and Hounds, but this was laughed to scorn among all but the children. Who would want to blow up the Fox and Hounds? The enemy would gain no advantage by that. A third theory, that the explosion had been caused by a secret weapon now coming into use, fired according to one school of thought from the North Pole and according to another from the interior of Germany by Hitler himself, wasn't given much credence either.

If it was a secret weapon, why should it be aimed at Lower Pupton? Lower Pupton contained no kind of military target. There were no military installations nearer than the Royal Aircraft Establishment at Farnborough. And so by a process of elimination everybody returned, for the time being at least, to the volcano theory, and the army which came down and prodded around and interrogated Josiah Tanner patiently and in detail made no attempt to deny that it was all the result of an eruption from the bowels of the earth.

Josiah himself, a thick, redfaced man who wore a strand of black hair pasted over his shiny and otherwise bare dome, was not able to shed much light on the matter.

He had been blown into Mrs. Green's victory garden and through falling in newly turned earth had sustained only minor injuries. Such an experience might have wrecked the nerves of a more highly strung individual. But Josiah was slow thinking and slow moving and was not to be overly put out by a volcanic eruption right under his public house.

Before a secret military board in Winchester, he carefully went over his story. He had closed up for the night at 10 P.M. in accordance with the requirements of the Defense of the Realm Act. At 9:50 P.M. he had said, "Last round, gentlemen, please," and served those who had wanted a drink. At 10 P.M. he had said, "Time, gentlemen, please! Time in the King's name!" and picked up the empty glasses. No, there hadn't been any strangers in the house. No. There was no guest. Yes, he lived all alone. He had locked up carefully, left some of the beer mugs in the sink and gone to his own quarters in the back of the barroom.

He had been feeling tired and looking forward to a nice hot bath. He had filled the bathtub and climbed in for a good soak. He reckoned that would be about 10:20. Then he had started washing himself. He always stood up and soaped himself all over and then sat down in the warm water. He liked to do it that way.

. Major de Saster, who was conducting the inquiry, grew impatient.

"Yes. Yes," he said. "I'm perfectly familiar with the normal techniques for bathing. What happened then?"

"Well," said Josiah, "I rinsed myself off proper and then reached down and I pulled out the plug—and the whole bloomin' building blew up."

That was all the light he could throw on the situation. At the precise moment that he pulled the plug out of the bottom of his bathtub, the building had disintegrated, hurling the pink, clean, nude Josiah several hundred feet through the air into Mrs. Green's victory garden and dirtying him all up again.

"Very interesting," said Major de Saster. "I trust, however, that this will not discourage you from bathing in the future." That closed the matter as far as his evidence was concerned, though Josiah, after pondering the whole incident, decided to file a claim for war damages just in case it hadn't been a volcano.

Mrs. Manners, however, was by no means satisfied with the volcano theory. Her active little mind was at work and her leaping imagination vaulted over great mountains of speculation. She recalled that Mrs. Searwood had thrust herself, Mrs. Wedge and Mrs. Skipton all down into the cellar after warning them that they were going to be bombed. From Mrs. Wedge and Mrs. Skipton she learned that while she, Mrs. Manners, had been in her trance Mrs. Searwood had asked, "What is this thing that is going to happen?" Only Mrs. Manners had convinced them both that what Mrs. Searwood had said was, "When is it going to happen?" This foreknowledge of the explosion, added to Mrs. Searwood's habit of talking to someone who wasn't there (a Nazi agent, she told herself, who was always hidden somewhere near her) and the evidence of the Berlin labels on Mrs. Searwood's baggage, convinced her that Mrs. Searwood was a German saboteur. This didn't fit in too well immediately with the theory that Mrs. Searwood was also the wife of Rudolph Hess. But it only took her a little while to evolve a beautiful new theory.

Mrs. Searwood was indeed the wife of Rudolph Hess, and Hitler was angry with her and her husband for flying to England and intent upon destroying her. However, Mrs. Searwood had managed to placate Hitler by promising to act as a saboteur, blowing up buildings all around England in the most unexpected places so as to strike terror in people everywhere and so help to win the war for Germany.

She tried the theory on her husband, who hummed and nodded all the way through it as he had hummed and nodded all the way through all her theories in the twenty years of their marriage. Then she tried it on Mrs. Wedge, and meeting with fertile ground here elaborated by pointing to Mrs. Searwood's remarkable demonstration as a marksman at the coconut shies.

"You've heard, of course, of the Germans' women's league haven't you, my dear?" she asked. "You know, they teach all their women to ride and wrestle and shoot and so on and some of them they say are better at it than men. Well, no man could throw a ball like that, but those Germans are awfully clever. I believe she got a thorough training by the Nazis. Probably for bomb throwing."

Mrs. Wedge bustled off to tell Mrs. Skipton, who snorted in disbelief though shaken at being reminded that Mrs. Searwood had warned them they were going to be bombed. She went up to Mrs. Searwood's room and looked at her luggage and there sure enough were the labels with *Berlin* marked on them as plain as day.

Mrs. Manners tried out her theory on so many people that she thought she ought in self-defense to tell the military of it, and her husband encouraged her to do this in the hope that they would choke her off. He liked Mrs. Searwood himself and didn't believe a word of his wife's theories. So Mrs. Manners took the bus in to Winchester and after worrying and harrying a platoon of orderlies was finally admitted to the presence of Major de Saster.

There she laid the whole story before him, with great stress on the German labels and the foreknowledge of the bombing, though she left out all mention of the séance since Major de Saster did not impress her as a man who was spiritually inclined. She did, however, dwell upon Mrs. Searwood's remarkable skill at the coconut shies as proof positive that she had belonged to some Nazi women's league whose members were trained to throw bombs around corners. And for good measure she threw in Mrs. Searwood's activities in getting work started on the restoration of St. Cedric's window. This, she explained, was merely to divert suspicion from herself.

By the time she was through, Major de Saster had concluded that all the village idiots in England had been moved for the duration of the war to Lower Pupton le Soeur. First there was that blockhead Tanner who thought you could blow up an inn by pulling the plug out of a bathtub, then there was this woman with her wild theory about Rudolph Hess's wife, when Hess, as far as he knew, wasn't even married. And then there was this Searwood woman who did tricks with balls at coconut shies.

Patiently he told Mrs. Manners to say nothing more about it for the present and that he would look into it. The trouble was that orders had come through from headquarters for the fullest report on the explosion with more than a hint that the Prime Minister was personally interested in it. He contented himself with sending a corporal over to interview Mrs. Searwood, and the corporal returned with a report that Mrs. Searwood seemed like a nice old lady, a bit off the beam, who kept talking to herself and had solemnly assured him that the bomb was aimed at her because of something she had said in Berlin some years back about the Germans being dirty people.

Major de Saster prudently decided not to make any mention of Mrs. Manners or Mrs. Searwood in his report. He did, however, have the corporal call on Mrs. Manners to warn her once again about making any further mention of her theories.

The damage was, however, done.

Slowly the village, which had at first welcomed Mrs. Searwood, turned against her. Mrs. Wedge stopped dropping in for chats. Mrs. Skipton was almost perfunctory in getting her meals. Even Mrs.

Manners, when Mrs. Searwood dropped in at the grocery, served her in silence without any attempts at questioning, and when others were there all conversation would cease on Mrs. Searwood's entry, to be resumed as soon as she left.

None of them said anything directly to her. It was too appalling a thing to accuse someone, even a stranger, to their face of wanting to blow up the village. But behind her back the whole village buzzed with a dozen variations of the story that Mrs. Searwood was a German saboteur, and the visit of Major de Saster's corporal to Mrs. Manners helped to feed the fires of suspicion she had kindled. Where once Mrs. Searwood had been something of a social prize, eagerly sought for teas and whist drives, now she was shunned. The work on St. Cedric's window again came to a halt because nobody wanted to be associated with a project in which Mrs. Searwood had a hand.

Even Parson Pendlebury, who continued to call on her despite the gossip which had reached his ears too, was troubled. He did not believe a scrap of it for a moment, and chided his parishioners privately and in sermons on the evils of calumny and detraction. But they decided he was biased in her favor and paid little attention to his homilies. He did not want, any more than anyone else, to broach the matter directly to Mrs. Searwood, telling her of the dreadful suspicions he had heard voiced about her activities. But it hurt him that she should be so treated, and that the splendid work on the window should be put aside. He felt that unless she did something to fully clear her name, the village would never trust her again, and St. Cedric might never smile once more through the stained-glass window of his tiny church upon the villagers of whom he was the patron saint. It was she who had got the work of restoration started and only she who had the drive to get it finished.

One day, after several dozen imaginary late cuts to the boundary in his garden while he turned the whole thing over in his mind, he called on Mrs. Searwood and asked her outright whether she knew anything at all, however insignificant, of the explosion.

"Not a thing," said Mrs. Searwood, "except that that Hitler hasn't given me a moment's rest since the war started. He bombed my apartment in London, sent an airplane after me in Kensington

High Street in broad daylight, and found out where my furniture was stored and blew up the warehouse. And now he's found that I'm living in Lower Pupton and is after me here. I know that you won't believe that," she added, for this was the first time she had mentioned her feud with Hitler to the parson. "But I'm used to not being believed. However, I know what I'm talking about. I've been the target of more of Hitler's bombs than any individual in the whole of England. *My* apartment bombed out of three hundred apartments in the same building. *My* furniture blown to smithereens of all the furniture stored in that warehouse. And now this explosion in one insignificant little village in England to which I have come for sanctuary.

"But I'm not going to take it lying down any more. Priscilla (that's my daughter you know) asked me to leave the war to the Army and the Americans in the past and I did so, and a lot of good it has done. I'm going to find out what's at the bottom of this thing, and when I do I'm going to take the whole story to the Prime Minister himself. He'll know how to deal with the matter."

Her vehemence startled Parson Pendlebury. Fond of her as he was, he couldn't quite subscribe to the theory that the whole war revolved around a personal feud between Mrs. Searwood and Hitler because of some remarks she had made in Berlin. And yet he had to admit that there was a chain of hazard connected with her which suggested something more than coincidence. He contented himself with offering to drive her to Winchester or anywhere else she wished if she had anything at all to tell the authorities, and then left.

The ill-concealed hostility of the village, mounting now for a week, was beginning to tell on Mrs. Searwood's normally sunny nature. It upset her badly to get little more than "Good morning" out of the talkative Mrs. Wedge when they met, and little more than "Yes" or "No" out of Mrs. Skipton, and she took her troubles to Chief White Feather.

She knew that she had fallen from grace, but could not understand why since nobody had even hinted of the true cause to her.

"You'd think that I'd blown up their silly pub the way they're treating me," she complained. "They never even stop to ask themselves just what I stand to gain by destroying the only source of French brandy in five miles."

"Well, they *do* think you've blown up their silly pub as you call it," said Chief White Feather.

"They *what?*" said Mrs. Searwood, in complete astonishment.

"They think you blew the Fox and Hounds up. I thought you knew. Mrs. Manners started the whole story with her theory that you're Rudolph Hess's wife. All this suspicion that's attached to you, of which I thought you knew already, is of course nothing but ignorance and nonsense. Still it conforms nicely with well-established patterns of human psychology. There is nothing truer about mass reaction than that the alien always receives the blame for disaster. I recall, during my studies of medieval history of Europe, that the Black Death was blamed upon the Jews, it being claimed that they were poisoning wells and food all over Europe. Thousands of them were burned alive although the facts point to infection by the Suljek Turks crossing . . ."

"I don't care about the Suljek Turks," snapped Mrs. Searwood, "and although I'm sorry about the Jews that doesn't help me in Lower Pupton. Just what do you mean that Mrs. Manners started this? Has she been going around the place telling everybody that I blew up the Fox and Hounds?"

Chief White Feather explained the whole of Mrs. Manners's elaborate theory about her, and as she listened Mrs. Searwood grew white with anger. "I'll go right down and see that woman this very instant," she said, "and have the whole thing out with her. Where's my hat? The very idea."

"That won't do the slightest bit of good," said White Feather. "It will only add to the gossip. Mrs. Manners will deny ever saying a word and then where will you be? Just forget about it and it will all blow over in time."

"I will *not* forget about it," retorted Mrs. Searwood. "I won't have my good name mixed up with a public house for one thing, even if it did blow up. I'm going to find out about that explosion if it's the last thing I do. And I'm going to confront that Mrs. Manners with the whole story. She's just a mean, nasty woman—a medium.

That's what you get for associating with spirits." Chief White Feather winced. "And," continued Mrs. Searwood illogically, "I wish you'd do something to help me instead of sitting there and giving me a lecture on mass psychology and the Suljek Turks and Jews. You men are so useless."

Chief White Feather gave her a hard, almost bitter look.

"You do me an injustice," he said. "I have been doing something about it. I got tired of trying to teach Old Grady chess, and the explosion, of a nature such as I have not experienced before, naturally presented itself as a challenge both to my intellect and my extensive education. So I have been working on the problem for some days and have come up with an intriguing solution. In fact, I believe I can now claim to know everything about it." He lapsed into silence intended both to give drama to his statement and serve as a rebuke to Mrs. Searwood for her attitude.

"You know all about it?" cried Mrs. Searwood. "You mean to tell me that you've found out all about this explosion and you've sat there preening yourself on your superior intelligence and let all those people say those horrid things about me, and snub me and . . ." She put her head in her hands and burst into tears.

"My dear, my dear," said Chief White Feather, in deep concern. "Don't take on so. I had no idea that all this village talk would affect you so badly. If I had as much as suspected . . ."

"Oh, it's all right," said Mrs. Searwood, blowing her nose and wiping her eyes behind her glasses. "It's just the thought of what everybody has been thinking about me, and Parson Pendlebury too. I've been leading up to a good cry for a long time and all this—all this nastiness has brought it on, that's all. I've got to clear my name somehow. Even Mr. Pendlebury doesn't believe that I'm innocent. I see that now. That's why he called the other day and started talking about the explosion instead of the window. I know he thinks I've got something to do with it too though he'd rather die than admit it." And she started to cry again.

"There, there," said Chief White Feather, "don't be upset. Remember all my degrees. We'll work out something. Look. I'll tell you all I've found out and maybe between the two of us we can work out a way to clear you." Mrs. Searwood dried her eyes and after a sob or two more was ready to listen.

"Here's what I know," said Chief White Feather. "I'll be brief because it's all rather technical. Now as a result of examining the crater and the dispersal of the debris, and calculations based on the parabola described by Mr. Tanner from his bathtub into Mrs. Green's victory garden, I've been able to discover the angle of impact of the missile (for it was a missile), the approximate amount of TNT detonated, and the type of projectile used—a projectile which I might add was a humdinger."

"You found out all that by just looking at the crater?" asked Mrs. Searwood incredulously.

"Oh, lots more. Those are the mere elements," replied Chief White Feather. He could not resist a little preening. "One does not graduate from Oxford and Cambridge several hundred times in the course of three centuries without amassing a certain amount of knowledge, popular concepts to the contrary. But to return to the subject. Estimating the weight of the good Mr. Tanner, the distance of his bathtub from the center of the explosion and the distance he went through the air gave me a fairly good figure on the amount of TNT used—about fifty pounds. Not enough for an aerial bomb and too much for a shell. So the missile, I suspected, was of a completely new kind.

"A few other circumstances gave me a clue to its true character. For instance, nobody in Lower Pupton, irrespective of where situated at the time of the explosion, heard any sound before the blast. However, some seconds after the blast they heard sounds which they varyingly described to each other as a shrill whistle and a loud rustle."

"And what does that mean?" asked Mrs. Searwood.

"Well, the missile was traveling faster than the sound it made passing through the air. It was traveling faster than sound, in other words, or faster than about six hundred and sixty miles an hour, though the speed of sound varies, as you undoubtedly know, according to atmospheric conditions."

Mrs. Searwood did not know, but she nodded her head anyway. Her knowledge of physics was limited to a vague story about lighting a candle and going around the world seven and a half times in one second.

"Now," continued White Feather, who was walking up and down, one hand behind his back, lecturing like a don, "you will remember that I said the sound—a whistle or a rustle—was heard *several* seconds after the explosion. That would suggest that the missile was traveling very much faster indeed than the speed of sound—perhaps twice as fast. No shell is capable of maintaining such a speed, certainly not at the end of its trajectory. Neither is a bomb, which relies for its motive power on the force of gravity. That suggested to me, indeed it made it plain, that the projectile was neither a bomb nor a shell but a rocket."

"A rocket?" said Mrs. Searwood.

"A rocket," said Chief White Feather. "A huge rocket. The only problem left to solve was where it came from. That was easiest of all—a mere matter of arriving at its weight and tracing its flight through the air by means of a slight calculation involving gravity, air temperature, humidity, curvature of the earth with an allowance for wind drift . . ."

"How did you find out how much it weighed when it was all blown to pieces?" asked Mrs. Searwood dubiously.

"Well, it's a little involved to explain," said Chief White Feather, "but for a rocket with a warhead of two thousand one hundred pounds, you'd need about seven thousand six hundred pounds of alcohol and eleven thousand pounds of liquid oxygen as a fuel to drive it across the Channel to Lower Pupton. I had to assume that it came from the Continent. It could have come from an enemy warship or a submarine, but those are pretty remote possibilities. It's far more likely that it was launched from land. To hold that amount of fuel and the mechanism to control its burning my calculations demand a rocket about forty-seven feet high, five feet in diameter and weighing twelve tons. It's really quite simple once you know how to go about it. Without going into too many details the unavoidable conclusion is that the Fox and Hounds was blown up by the explosion of a big rocket launched about fifty miles inside of France at a point SSE by ½ E of Lower Pupton."

He paused to let this sink in and then added slowly. "There'll probably be lots more of them. Once you know how to make a weapon like that, it is not difficult to make hundreds more. And this is one device your antiaircraft defenses can't do anything about. These rockets travel too fast to shoot down or intercept in any way. Once they're launched, there's nothing on earth can stop them landing. The only thing to do is to destroy them at the launching site."

"This is much more serious than I thought," exclaimed Mrs. Searwood. "It isn't any longer just a matter of clearing my name. People are in danger of being blown to bits all over the place. Nothing will be safe—not even St. Cedric's window. Oh, how dreadful if they were to smash that to smithereens. We must go to London this very moment and see the Prime Minister and tell him all about it.

"My dear Mrs. Searwood," said Chief White Feather, "I don't want to underestimate the force of your rather remarkable personality, but do you really think—even if you could get to see the Prime Minister—that he would believe what you told him?

"Consider the whole circumstances. What can you say? That the explosion in Lower Pupton of which he probably has the fullest details by now, was caused by a huge rocket launched from France? That's fine. But what are you going to say when he asks you how you know this? That you were told by the spirit of an American Indian who is a multiple graduate of Oxford University?

"He just won't believe you. People don't believe in spirits except for short periods when they happen to be in an old cemetery around midnight. Just think for a second. If before you had met me someone had told you the same story, what would you have said of him?"

Mrs. Searwood had to agree that she would think such a person was out of his mind.

"And that's just what the Prime Minister would think of you," said White Feather. "Of course, I could write down all the calculations for you on twenty or thirty sheets of paper, and you could take them along with you. But that wouldn't help much. You couldn't pretend that you'd arrived at them yourself. They would trip you up easily. And you couldn't say you got them from me, because we have agreed they'd think you were out of your mind and wouldn't even bother to check them. And they might well come to the conclusion, if they did check the figures and found them accurate, that there was something fishy about the whole thing—that you really were in on it, but on the wrong side—and put you in the Tower."

"You're right," said Mrs. Searwood ruefully. "No one is regarded with so much suspicion in England as a woman with a scientific education. I've got to get some kind of proof that just can't be ignored."

"Why don't you forget about it?" said Chief White Feather. "The Army experts will be working on the problem and they'll probably arrive at the solution in a month or two."

"Yes," snapped Mrs. Searwood, "with half the people in England dead in the meantime and never knew what hit them. Besides, you seem to forget that I'm personally involved in this. I'm not going to stay here doing nothing with everybody thinking me a murderer and a pro-Nazi until the Army finds out about this rocket. There must be some way we can convince the Prime Minister about it."

"Well," said White Feather, dubiously, "if you really want to get proof that cannot be ignored, I know of a way, but I can't say that I recommend it."

"What is it?"

"Quite simple, really. We could steal a reconnaissance plane from the airfield, fly to France and get some pictures of the rockets and rocket sites. They can't argue with pictures taken in one of their own sealed cameras from one of their own airplanes."

"Don't be silly," said Mrs. Searwood petulantly. "I can't fly an airplane."

"Well, I can," said White Feather, warming to his own suggestion. "I've followed the development of aviation closely ever since the first cross-Channel flight by Bleriot. It's been one of my hobbies. As a matter of fact, I've made several important contributions in the field of aeronautical research myself. Of course, others got the credit, claiming that they had an inspiration that suddenly flashed into their minds. They never stopped to consider who put it there in the first instance. Human beings are very egoistical. It took me several years of spiritual suggestion to educate English designers to the point where they were prepared to drop the biplane in favor of the monoplane. I have several excellent plans for airplanes with swept-back wings and an entirely revolutionary method of propulsion which I keep trying to put across but the innate British conservatism is exceedingly difficult to deal with and makes me wonder at times that the British ever decided to trust themselves to the air at all."

Mrs. Searwood was very dubious about the whole project. She had never been in an airplane in her life. She felt that only a very special kind of person—a sort of new type of human being—was capable of handling one. And she was not at all sure, and said so, that Chief White Feather was not bragging about being able to fly.

"My dear lady," said White Feather somewhat put out by her doubts, "what do you suppose I was doing during the Battle of Britain? Recollect, I beg you, that I have been in this country for three hundred years, and although not a British subject, became exceedingly fond of the British people, whose wars and battles I have followed for three centuries in my studies of military science.

"Do you imagine that a spirit who had witnessed the magnificent stand of the Guards at Waterloo, holding their section of the line against overwhelming odds for several hours; who saw the farmers of Cromwell's army at Marston Moor rebuff some of the best troops in Europe; who saw Nelson lay the *Victory*, her decks nothing but carnage, alongside the *Redoubtable* at Trafalgar—do you imagine that such a spirit could stand by and take no part in such a splendid action?"

"You mean," said Mrs. Searwood, astonished, "that you helped the RAF during the Battle of Britain? I thought it was gremlins."

"Gremlins, fiddlesticks," retorted White Feather. "Nothing but superstitious nonsense, the result of a peculiar British habit of attributing personality and life to inanimate objects. It dates back to the Saxon reverence for stones, trees, rivers and so on. Quite apart from my warm feelings for the British people, I saw in the Battle of Britain an enormous intellectual challenge, an occasion that could not fail to fascinate any student of the science of war.

"Consider the new ramparts which were being assaulted. No longer the Channel cliffs and shores, but the very air. Consider how few were the defenders and how small their resources. And how many were the attackers. They came like locusts from every quarter. And the little moths of Spitfires and Hurricanes leapt from the ground to challenge them, circling in and out, and I among them, seeing that guns did not jam and repairing controls that were shot away.

"What a splendid occasion it was, for if a man must die and die young what better way is there than over his own homeland defending the ground that nurtured him and all his ancestors? They fell like stars and died like Vikings, but they took more than their own number with them. Over one hundred and eighty planes in one day I recall, and I rode the wind with them and indeed so far forgot my cultural background as to shout the ancient war-cries of my race, standing on the wing of a Spitfire and closing with the enemy."

He lapsed into silence, engrossed in his memories. Mrs. Searwood was remembering too, remembering the great dark city like a crouching beast, the searchlights slicing the blackness of the sky to ribbons, the far-off chatter of machine guns and cannon and then the flaming planes falling down as if some piece of the fabric of the heavens had caught fire and was plunging to earth.

"Well," she said at length, "I do believe that you can fly an airplane. But that's only the beginning of the problem. How are we going to get one? You can't just walk into an airfield and take a plane away. They're all carefully counted no doubt, and one would be missed immediately."

"You let me worry about that," said White Feather. "The point is, do you feel deeply enough about this to want to take the risk?"

Mrs. Searwood thought it over for a minute and then said, firmly, that she did. It seemed the only way she would be able to clear her name with the village and Parson Pendlebury, and, more important, convince the Prime Minister about the rockets and save all the people who might become victims of them.

"All right," said White Feather. "Arrange for Parson Pendlebury to drive you to Farnborough Royal Aircraft Establishment tomorrow night at 10. Then get rid of him. I'll meet you there at the main gate to the airfield. We'll have to wait around awhile until nearer dawn, but if you ask him to take you to the airfield any later, he'll get suspicious and may spoil the whole thing."

CHAPTER THIRTEEN

"SEE HERE," said Chief White Feather to Old Grady, "I've got something for you to do that is right up your alley."

Old Grady bobbed, as eager as a schoolboy anticipating a half-day holiday. Anything at all would be a welcome relief from White Feather's daily and merciless drilling in the fundamentals of chess. He had long ago despaired of ever learning it. There were too many different kinds of pieces involved, each with their own moves and he couldn't understand why a castle should be permitted to move at all. Then the game lacked the very essentials of sport because you couldn't cheat at it. He had tried and had received a harsh tongue-lashing from White Feather.

"Yes sir," said Old Grady. He had an enormous respect for the Indian, and this amused White Feather, who recalled that the reverse had been true when Old Grady's contemporaries had first met Chief White Feather's ancestors in the New World.

"You've been selected," he said, "for a position of trust. You have always been wanting someone to trust you, and Mrs. Searwood has decided to do so in a very important matter indeed. One upon which her whole future may depend." Old Grady doted on Mrs. Searwood with the fondness of an ancient spaniel, and smiled in gratitude at the thought that she was going to trust him.

"I won't let her down," he said eagerly. "I won't let her down if it costs me my life."

"You seem to forget you're already dead," said White Feather. "But never mind. Now listen carefully. Here's what you have to do.

117

You're to do some haunting." (Old Grady's smile expanded now into one of ecstasy.) "You'll come with me to the main gate of the RAE at Farnborough. Mrs. Searwood will be there and we have to get her inside past the sentry. You have to haunt the sentry. Stand off to the side and make your noises. Make them sound really agonizing, so that he thinks somebody is dying near by. When he goes to investigate, Mrs. Searwood will slip through. You understand?"

"Yes," said Old Grady, "I do. And you can trust me. I know nobody has been able to trust me before. But you can trust me this time. And if I do all right, then I'll be able to go away and live among the other spirits, won't I?"

"Yes," said Chief White Feather, "you will. This is your big chance."

"I'm ready," said Old Grady. "Oooooer. Oooooooer."

"Cut that out," said White Feather. "You don't have to haunt me. Just the sentry. Come along."

THE OFFICIAL RECORDS on the matter have been destroyed. They were destroyed at the instigation of the Secretary of State for Air and they were destroyed for a very good reason. It is essential that all branches of the armed services take themselves and their doings seriously. It is essential that they develop and retain a dignity which will not permit of levity in their official proceedings. It is above all essential that if any levity, or irregularity, of an unseemly nature does creep into their official proceedings, that it be expunged without mercy lest it come to the ears of an irreverent press and provoke embarrassing questions in Parliament.

For these reasons, Air Marshal Noble called in all the records on the theft of an armed Mustang reconnaissance plane from the Royal Aircraft Establishment at Farnborough in the early morning of May 13, 1944, read them through page by page (there were two hundred and thirteen pages plus one hundred and twenty-four pages of statements from witnesses) and then burned them one by one in the grate of his private office.

As he burned them his anger mounted and his wrath reached its peak when on page 116 he read the verbatim statement of Aircraftsman Second Class John Spender which ran as follows:

"On the morning of May 13, 1944, I was on sentry duty at the north gate of the airfield. I came on duty at 0400 hours and was to be relieved at 0800 hours.

"I was sober, not having taken any alcoholic beverages since the morning of April 30, 1944, when the canteen ran out of beer. My post comprised the immediate area of the gate which is back of the plane hangars, and my instructions were to march twenty paces across the gate, about-turn and march back again, repeating this every three minutes until relieved or given contrary instructions.

"The gate is a small one, big enough only for foot traffic and cut for the convenience of pilots in leaving the field as otherwise they have to walk a mile and a half to the main gate to get to the Mucky Duck. [NOTE: Aircraftsman Second Class Spender was apparently referring to the White Swan tavern.—O/C Investigations.]

"At 0500 hours, I thought I heard a noise at the far end of my beat. It sounded like someone blowing into an empty bottle. At first I took no notice but the noise seemed to approach me and increase in intensity and then go away, leading to a place fifteen paces past the gate. I thought it was one of them Yanks up to their tricks, but I could see no one. I gave the regular challenge as laid down in King's Regulations. There was no reply but the noise continued and grew louder and was accompanied by what seemed to be the sound of chains rattling.

"I decided to investigate and put my rifle at the ready and walked over to the place where the noise was coming from. It seemed to be all around me and fair gave me the creeps but I couldn't find anything except an old boot, size twelve. [NOTE: The boot in question was subsequently examined and found to be the variety used by farm laborers in the district. There were no noise-making devices hidden in it.—O/C Investigations.]

"I had decided to call the corporal when I saw someone that looked like a little old lady run through the gate. She scurried over to one of the planes outside the hangar, climbed into the cockpit, started the engine and took off. The noise then ceased and I called the corporal.

"And that's the truth, so help me God."

"Confounded nonsense," roared Air Marshal Noble and hurled the whole monstrous document into the grate, stabbing it viciously with the poker.

ONCE INSIDE THE PLANE, Chief White Feather told Mrs. Searwood to sit still and touch nothing. "Goodness," said Mrs. Searwood in dismay, "there's only room for one of us."

"If you'll think back to your broom closet in London," White Feather replied, "you'll recall that we spirits require no physical room." He slipped in beside her and pressed down the starter switch; the propeller turned over slowly at first, then with a mounting whine until the engine commenced coughing and choking and then roared into life. He revved it up, noted that the oil pressure was satisfactory, the fuel gauge full. Then, when it seemed that the noise had reached a crescendo which it would be impossible to exceed without everything falling to pieces, he took off the brake and the plane slipped down the runway and off and up into the dawn.

Mrs. Searwood, through all this, kept her eyes shut on the theory that if there was going to be some violence either to the plane or herself, it might not be quite so bad if she didn't look at it. When she opened her eyes, the noise had quieted down and she discovered that they were already a thousand feet in the air and the airport was receding rapidly beneath them. The dawn light was beginning to seep across the land from the east, throwing grotesque shadows from trees and buildings below. Over to the west there was no light at all and she realized with a thrill that here she was suspended between day and night. It was daylight far away to the left of the plane and night to the right and she thought how strange it was to be flying along the very rim of the dawn.

When the plane took off, she had had a sensation of weight pressing down on all parts of her body, but now that was gone and she had instead a feeling of lightness. Her spasm of terror at seeing herself above the ground, the solid familiar earth which she had never left in all her days, began to give way slowly to a kind of exuberance. She couldn't quite account for this but it seemed to be related to the novel experience of being above the surface of the world. Down below were all the troubles and cares which she had experienced from the time she was a little girl. But up here was a new and unexplored element, indeed a new world, which somehow seemed so removed from trouble that it made her feel carefree for the first time since the rocket had fallen on Lower Pupton.

"I like this," she said. "So long as I don't look down I feel wonderful. It's like getting completely away from everything—as if the world didn't really exist at all. I don't ever want to go back to it."

"That's the way we spirits feel," said Chief White Feather. "When we were alive we didn't want to die at all, despite all our troubles. But when we had died, physically that is, it was so completely different from what we expected that it's laughable we should have been in such fear of our mortal end. Just like being in a new world, as you feel now."

"I'm not dead, am I?" asked Mrs. Searwood with some anxiety.

"Oh no," replied Chief White Feather, "you're still alive, and unfortunately you have to return to earth in a few hours. But enjoy it while you can.

"By the way, you'll have to take over flying this thing in a while, because I must look over the camera and see how it works and I've got to do some navigating too. There's about a fifteen-mile-an-hour cross-wind, so we'll have to fly about one hundred and seventy-three degrees by my reckoning. See that line there?" (He pointed to the lubber line in the aerial compass.) "Well, keep it on one hundred and seventy-three degrees. Look, I'll show you how to fly this, though it's a little different from a Spitfire. I took the Mustang—an American job—because the Spits are not armed when used for reconnaissance. On a trip like this we're likely to get into a scramble and I didn't want to take any risks with you along.

"Flying is really very simple if you don't think about it. It's an emotion, not a mental effort. It's done by feeling rather than by reason. It isn't a thing to think about. If you think too much, you'll fly badly."

"I know," said Mrs. Searwood, "it's like riding a bicycle. Ronnie Briggs told me."

"Well, in a way," said White Feather. "Now here's what to do. Those two pedals under your feet are for steering with. The one on the left steers the plane to the left and the one on the right to the right. Try pressing one of them gently." Mrs. Searwood pressed the left one and the plane skidded around on a new course.

"Fine," said White Feather. "Now press the other one and when the needle comes back to one hundred and seventy-three keep it there." It took several minutes of aerial gyration, but eventually Mrs. Searwood managed it.

"You're doing splendidly," said Chief White Feather. "Now this stick in the middle here is the control column. If you press it forward the plane goes down and if you pull it back, it starts to go up. Pull it back slowly." Mrs. Searwood did so and the Mustang clawed up into the sky.

"Excellent," said Chief White Feather, "now ease it forward." Mrs. Searwood pushed the stick away from her rather quickly and the earth tilted up in front of them and rushed toward the plane.

At that moment, as they sped toward the earth another plane snarled over the top, its guns blazing, banked and swept up into the sky above.

"Oh. Oh," said Chief White Feather, "here comes trouble."

He took the controls from Mrs. Searwood, pulled back on the stick and gave the plane full throttle. The Mustang soared upward with the ease and grace of a swallow. Chief White Feather looked around anxiously overhead. "That's another Mustang," he said. "In fact, another armed reconnaissance plane. They had several of them at Farnborough for experiment. The pilot was probably sent out to get us down and grabbed the first plane handy. I'm going to have to get into a cloud in a hurry. That boy apparently means business."

To the left, and perhaps ten miles away, he spotted a thick formation of cloud and headed towards it. He reckoned it would take two minutes, perhaps two and a half, to make it. It offered, he knew, only a temporary haven but at least would give him time to think out his next move. The distance lessened rapidly and then with only a minute more to go and the cloud enticingly near, the other plane dove out of the east toward them—almost invisible with the sun behind it.

RONNIE BRIGGS WAS ANNOYED that he had missed with his first burst. His orders were to shoot down the stolen Mustang, which he concluded had been taken by a spy or perhaps an escaped German Luftwaffe officer, and he intended on this his first combat mission in his own plane to do just that with a minimum waste of time.

He had circled up behind and then dived but just as he got his sights lined up and pressed the firing button, the plane ahead, obviously flown by an experienced combat pilot, streaked for the ground. If it had gone up, he could have followed it readily, but diving he had overshot and Ronnie grinned for it was a good trick.

He banked, circled, saw the stolen plane headed for a cloud formation and streaked off to get between it and the sun and make another pass. He had just a matter of seconds on his side but this time he was sure of the kill. He flipped his Mustang over in a half turn and roll and came in. And then, just as he was about to press the firing button again, something about the look of the pilot in the other plane, something familiar about the contour of the head, recognized in a twinkling, made him hesitate. The other pilot was apparently either wearing a peculiar white flying helmet or had a head of flowing white hair. Instead of firing he swooped over the top and peering down below saw one standard Mustang, with the familiar RAF markings, in perfect trim and nicely controlled and piloted apparently by Mrs. Martha Searwood, an elderly lady he had met only a week or so ago at Parson Pendlebury's garden party, and who had seemed more than ordinarily interested in flying.

"There's something wrong with me," he said soberly. "I'm having hallucinations."

He shut his eyes and the cloud swallowed both planes. Out on the other side he looked again. Yes, that's who it was. Mrs. Martha Searwood with the white hair and the pleasant motherly face sitting there with her town coat around her—the one with the bit of black fur on the collar—the stick held expertly in one negligent hand, flying like a veteran.

"What the hell am I supposed to do about this," he demanded of his airplane. "I can't shoot down Mrs. Searwood. I've got the rest of my life to live and I can't live it happily after shooting down a nice old lady from eleven thousand feet. And if I don't shoot her down, they'll throw me in the poky and leave me there until I'm old enough to be her father. Maybe I've gone batty. Maybe she isn't really there. Maybe it's just those powdered eggs I had for breakfast."

He slipped alongside and looked again, but it was Mrs. Searwood all right. She had let go the stick and was waving at him with both hands. He'd been flying for ten months now and still felt nervous about letting go the stick at eleven thousand feet and three hundred and sixty miles an hour.

"I've been bad all my life," Ronnie told his plane. "I've lived rough and enjoyed it. And now here's my punishment—clean out of my mind in an airplane two miles above the earth. Maybe I'm not in an airplane. Maybe this old bucket isn't here at all and I'm flying around in my pyjamas with a broomstick between my legs."

He patted his instrument board and was genuinely relieved to find that it was solid. He looked over at Mrs. Searwood again and saw that she was putting on her radiophones. She plugged them in expertly and her voice came over motherly and calm.

"Hello Ronnie," she said, "fancy meeting you here."

"Mrs. Searwood," said Ronnie, "you took the words right out of my mouth. Look, Mrs. Searwood, I know you like to fly airplanes. I remember your asking me at Parson Pendlebury's about flying Spits and so on. And you make a wizard pilot. Doing top-hole. I don't know how you do it. But Mrs. Searwood, my orders are to shoot you down and I don't want to because you're a nice old lady. Now, why don't you turn round and follow me back to the airfield. Maybe we can get you off with twenty years in the Tower, with time off for good behavior. How about it?"

"No Ronnie," said Mrs. Searwood, "I'm not going back. I've got something to do and I need this plane to do it with. It's very important."

"But Mrs. Searwood," Ronnie pleaded, "if I don't bring you back or shoot you down, they'll throw *me* in the Tower and I'm younger than you are and can't afford to waste the time. Pretend you're my mother and look at it from my point of view."

Mrs. Searwood didn't reply right away and Ronnie looked over at her in an attitude of prayer, his hands clasped together. His plane commenced to veer off to the left and he had to pull it back into position. It annoyed him to see that Mrs. Searwood was apparently piloting hers as steady as a rock without using her hands.

"No Ronnie," she said at length, "I can't go back yet, even if it does mean you have to go to jail. And if you have to shoot me down, go ahead. But it would be more sensible if you came along with me in case we meet any Germans. Do you remember when the Fox and Hounds blew up in Lower Pupton?"

"Yes," said Ronnie.

"Well, everybody thinks I did it but I didn't."

"I believe you didn't, Mrs. Searwood," Ronnie said. "Honest I do. Don't run away from them. I'll stand by you. When they've put you in the Tower I'll go right down to Lower Pupton and tell them you didn't have a single thing to do with blowing up the Fox and Hounds."

"Silly boy. It isn't that. The fact is that I know who did blow up the Fox and Hounds. Or rather, I know what blew it up. It was a huge rocket launched from France by the Nazis and there are lots more of them there. They fly at a speed faster than sound. They could blow up the whole of London. And I'm going over to get some pictures of them to show to the Prime Minister. That's why I took the airplane."

"Oh no," groaned Ronnie. "Not to get pictures of rockets in France that fly faster than sound and are designed to blow up public houses in England. Not that. Don't tell me that's what you stole one of His Majesty's blinking lend-lease airplanes for?"

"You see," said Mrs. Searwood, "that proved my point. You don't believe that there are such rockets, do you?"

"Not to put too fine a point on it," said Ronnie, "no."

"Nobody else would have either," said Mrs. Searwood. "That's what I had to borrow the plane for. To get pictures of them. It's a serious matter. If I can't convince the Prime Minister, everybody's liable to be blown up at any minute. I really had no choice. Now. Are you going to come along with me and see for yourself, or are you going to shoot me down?"

"Twenty years," said Ronnie. "What's twenty years? I'll only be forty-three. Lots of fellows don't get married until they're forty-three. Maybe Christine will wait for me. Maybe when she's forty-three I won't want to marry her anyway. Maybe she wouldn't marry me at twenty-three if I told her that on my first solo combat mission I shot down a nice old lady who wanted to go for a ride in an airplane to take some pictures. Lots of people want to take pictures from airplanes. It's natural. Everybody's normal. It's just me that's crazy.

"Okay, Ace, I can't shoot you down and I can't get you to turn back. So I'll just tag along behind your left wing and you tell me what to do. I'm just a green pilot with the best years of my life behind me and the longest ahead."

"That's a nice boy, Ronnie," said Mrs. Searwood. "I'll never forget you for this. Now do you have a camera on your plane?"

"Yep," said Ronnie. He was feeling a little lightheaded. "I've got a camera, lots of ammo, lots of gas and a flask of coffee. Let's go on a picnic and have a jolly time."

"This is no time for joking," said Mrs. Searwood severely, "I'm going to take pictures of those rockets from this plane but I want you to come in behind me and take some too in case I get shot down or anything goes wrong."

"Roger, Ace," said Ronnie. "Anything you say." He did a roll and then tagged in meekly behind the end of her wing, like a small boy who had shown too much exuberance on being taken for a walk by his nurse.

CHAPTER FOURTEEN

BELOW, THE CHANNEL GLEAMED like a strip of tinfoil, its waves marked by the tiniest of dark lines which Mrs. Searwood noted were moving up the body of water instead of towards the shore. She was surprised at this. She knew that waves rolled up the beaches and she had reasoned that since they rolled up the beaches of France which were opposite to the beaches of England, there must be a parting in the middle, as in a well-combed head of hair. But she could see no parting of the waves and turned to Chief White Feather for an explanation.

"Why don't the waves part in the middle?" she asked.

"Don't bother me now," said White Feather. "I'm trying to fix our position. All that chasing around with that idiot Briggs has thrown us off course. We could have flown to the right spot immediately, but now I'm not sure of our precise position. There's a margin of error of slightly over forty-six miles so we'll have to make a sweep. Now listen carefully to what I say. I'm going to bring us down to treetop height over France. Then I'll have to hand the plane over to you while I attend to the camera. For goodness' sake, don't fiddle with anything when I do, and if you feel you've got to do something, pull back on the stick. That'll take us up in the air. If you push forward even the slightest bit, we'll be ploughing into the ground in a second. The thing to do is to look at the farthest horizon and aim for that. That will keep us parallel with the ground. Do you understand?"

Mrs. Searwood said that she understood that she had to fly at the horizon, and Chief White Feather considered this for a minute and said, "Yes, that's right."

"Now," he continued, "see this little button on the control column? That's the firing button. If anything gets in your way, just press that button and the guns will open up."

"All right," said Mrs. Searwood dubiously, "but I don't want to hurt anybody."

"Well, you won't have any choice," said Chief White Feather, "but don't let it bother you. It won't be anyone you know and it's next to impossible to be sorry about hurting someone you haven't even met and never will. That's what makes war feasible."

They were over France now and he flipped the Mustang down toward the earth, which rushed towards them, growing larger and larger like the skin of a balloon which was being blown up very fast. When the altimeter read two hundred feet he commenced to straighten out and the plane fled over treetops, fields, houses and roads, all of them hurtling into view and then streaking into oblivion to be replaced in an instant by more.

"Now," said White Feather, "just keep it like this while I attend to the camera."

Mrs. Searwood gingerly took the stick and put her feet lightly on the rudder controls. She kept her eyes strained just above the horizon, which fled from them as fast as they approached it. She was conscious of people below hurling themselves into ditches, farm animals scattering in fright and once saw, out of the tail of her eye, three trucks loaded with soldiers pile into a ditch as the plane streaked over them. She would have liked to look more leisurely at this activity, but dared not. They flew over a town, the spire of whose church towered for a fraction of a second above them, over a stretch of woodland, an expanse of orchards and then on to another wood or rather forest, for it stretched to the horizon and the plane bumped as it hit the denser air over the trees.

Then, off to the right, a clearing appeared—a sudden little piece of no-forest in the middle of the trees, like a deep pit of black in a carpet of green. They were past it in a minute but Chief White

Feather called out, "That looks like the place. Turn round and let's take a dekko."

Mrs. Searwood had forgotten how to turn. All she could remember was Chief White Feather's instruction that if she did anything with the control column at all, she was to pull it back. She pulled back on it. The earth and forest suddenly disappeared. Ahead was a clear blue sky, endless and empty. Mrs. Searwood was all mixed up. The Mustang was climbing now, at an acute angle, but she had an idea that it was going down; that the earth had suddenly changed places with the sky and was now suspended miraculously above them.

"I can't find the horizon anywhere," she complained, "and I've forgotten how to turn this thing around."

"Rev her up," shouted Chief White Feather. "You're going to do an inside loop. Give her the gun!"

Mrs. Searwood remembered about the gun and pressed the button on the stick. The machine guns barked and spat viciously. A dark object like a clumsily constructed fly suddenly swung into view. Then bits of it jerked themselves from it and the thing crumbled and fell towards the ground in a plume of smoke.

"Good heavens," said Chief White Feather. "You've just shot down a Messerschmitt."

Suddenly the earth appeared again in its right place below them.

"Let go that stick," yelled White Feather. He grabbed it from her and the Mustang, again at treetop height, sped over the forest once more. "Hold it there," said White Feather and turned to the camera controls. The clearing was dead ahead and White Feather turned the camera on and the film commenced to purr through it. They were past in a second, but in that second Mrs. Searwood caught sight, in the middle of the clearing, of a tall slim pencil of metal, its tip just a few feet below the tops of the trees.

"Look!" she cried. "The rocket!"

"Right," said the Indian, "and I got a good shot of it. But we'll go back for one more. Now look, pull that stick back, but gently." Mrs. Searwood did so and the forest floated easily downwards.

"That's fine," said Chief White Feather. "Now, press the stick over to the right and press on the right rudder pedal. Not hard now, gently does it." The plane swung around until it was headed back in the direction from which it had come.

"First class," said White Feather. "Press the stick forward easily and when we've got downstairs, bring it back to the middle again and hold it there." The plane floated down to the treetops once again and the clearing sped towards them. White Feather got the camera going once more. They could see the rocket plainly ahead of them directly in the plane's path. A group of soldiers clustered around an ack-ack gun opened fire with a string of bullets which stitched through the wing of Mrs. Searwood's plane. She pressed the firing button. She did this involuntarily—a purely defensive reflex action. A torrent of bullets streaked from the plane and this frightened her more so she pressed the firing button more firmly. People below scattered in all directions.

"Pull back," yelled White Feather, "pull back. Let's get out of here." Mrs. Searwood, her guns still chattering, pulled back and the plane swooped upwards. She caught a glimpse of two other planes streaking by, one with black crosses on its wings and the other apparently piloted by Ronnie Briggs. Their sudden appearance frightened her so much that she let go the firing button though still holding on to the stick. Ronnie's voice came excitedly over the earphones. "Leave this one to me," he cried. "Look back. Look behind you."

Mrs. Searwood tried to look behind her, not through the rearview mirror, but by turning around, and in so doing banked the plane sharply so that it swung completely around on its course. Dead ahead now lay another Nazi plane. But what worried her more than this was that the earth and sky had changed places again. From where she sat, the earth was above her head and the sky below, for in turning she had flipped her plane over on its back.

"Oh bother," she exclaimed, "everything's upside down again. I wish things would stay in their place."

"Never mind that," said Chief White Feather, "press that firing button." The guns chattered again. The plane started to tremble as

if being pounded by a rivet gun and Mrs. Searwood was surprised to see the instrument panel falling to bits in front of her. Suddenly the Mustang commenced to pitch and buck, and then below her (though she thought it was over her head, for she was still upside down) she saw the Nazi plummeting to the ground and a parachute blossom over the green fields.

"I'm getting so that I don't believe this," said White Feather shaking his head. "You've shot him down. That's your second plane. You're flying this flivver like a veteran."

"I'm feeling dizzy," complained Mrs. Searwood. "All the blood seems to be rushing into my head."

"The blood *is* rushing to your head," said the Indian, "because you're upside down. Here, let me get this plane back upright again." He took over the controls and flipped the fighter back right way up. "You've done everything that's needed," he said, "and you showed like a champion. Just relax now and I'll fly this thing back to safety."

"You all right Ace?" asked Ronnie over the radiophone.

"Yes, I think so," said Mrs. Searwood, weakly.

"Not hurt or anything?" His voice was anxious. "No. But all my clocks are broken."

"Your clocks?"

"Yes. The dial things in front of me."

"Oh. Well, I'll take the lead and you follow me in. What a scramble. You bagged two and I got mine. Nobody's ever going to believe this. They won't believe it if I swear to it on a stack of Bibles as high as Nelson's monument. It just is incredible but it happened. Say, is that crate of yours behaving all right?"

"Tell him the engine's missing and I think we're running out of gas," said Chief White Feather.

Mrs. Searwood repeated the message.

"Oh no!" said Ronnie, "you can't do that to me. You'll have to ditch over the Channel and then I'll have to go on and nobody will believe me. I won't do it. I won't land alone at Farnborough and say that an old lady shot up two Messerschmitts and took some pictures of a whacking big rocket after flying a plane into the heart of occupied France. They wouldn't give me a second hearing. They'd throw me in the loony bin in a strait jacket. I'm going to ditch with you. Channel's right ahead. I'll send out an SOS for a crash boat."

"Tell him he can't ditch," said White Feather urgently. "Ask him if he got any pictures of the rocket. He can't ditch because if he did, the film may be destroyed. These cameras are supposed to be watertight but it's too much of a risk to take. He's got to land with those pictures if he got any or otherwise the whole thing may be useless."

Ronnie said yes, he'd got some pictures. And when Mrs. Searwood told him he would have to go on and land to save the film he groaned.

"They won't believe me," he said, "even when they see the film they won't believe me."

"Oh yes they will," said Mrs. Searwood. "They'll believe you. You're the only hope we have now. So go on. Otherwise they'll throw me in what you call the loony bin too. Can't you see that you've got to land safely with the camera?"

"I suppose so," said Ronnie glumly, "but I'll have to talk fast when I get there. Coming back, mission unaccomplished, with a story about a woman old enough to be my mother flying an airplane and taking pictures of rockets. I'm for it, I am. I hope they don't stand me up against a wall and shoot me before they develop this film." He put in an emergency call to what he called the boy scouts—the crash-boat station—and then said, "They'll be on the lookout for you, but I'll stick with you and see you down safe and then take off for home."

The Channel was below now—blue and inviting in the early summer sunshine. Mrs. Searwood's plane was losing altitude rapidly, its engine coughing, starting and then stalling again. Chief White Feather made a rapid calculation and decided they'd land about eight miles off the Solent. They scanned the surface of the sea anxiously and at last saw a white scar streaking out from the English coast.

"That's it," said Ronnie. "You'd better set her down as near to the crash boat as you can. Hope the water isn't too cold. Happy landing."

"I'm going to glide her down," said White Feather. "You unhook the top of that cockpit and be ready to get out on the wing when we touch."

Ronnie waved and headed off for the shore as Chief White Feather eased the Mustang down toward the sea. Mrs. Searwood suddenly became aware that there were waves on it, not little wrinkles as they had appeared, but big long slow rollers. She got the top of the cockpit back and the roaring of the wind made it impossible to say anything more. The plane skimmed the top of a wave, then seemed suddenly to be flying through glue before it stopped dead. Mrs. Searwood scrambled out on the wing as the crash boat came alongside.

SUBLIEUTENANT JOHN SPENLOVE FOTHERINGAY still cannot get anyone to believe him and has more or less given up trying. Now and again, when the evening is well along, and people are in a mellow mood, he makes another effort, but without much hope of success.

"Did I ever tell you fellows about the time I picked an old lady out of a fast reconnaissance plane in the middle of the Channel?" he says tentatively.

"Have another drink, old chap. It's best to ignore things like that," is the usual reply. "Just nerves. Happen to anybody."

He tried once to get hold of the official report to prove his case. But the report had mysteriously disappeared, and he couldn't even find any trace of his logbook. He couldn't find any of his own crew as witnesses either because shortly afterwards they were all suddenly transferred to duty in the Falkland Islands.

Eventually he came to doubt the whole thing himself.

CHAPTER FIFTEEN

CHIEF WHITE FEATHER said he personally liked the Tower, and Mrs. Searwood had to admit that it wasn't as bad as she thought it would be.

She had what amounted to a small apartment to herself in one of the walls overlooking the river. The window was very small and there were bars in front of it and she didn't like that. But the furniture—some chairs, a writing table and bed—was quite comfortable, and every day a matron came and took her for a bath. Her little apartment and the bathroom she used were quite high up, and she wondered who had to pump the water for it. She was quite sure that someone had to pump it, but the matron would not tell her anything. She presumed that some of the more hardened criminals had been given this task.

She had been taken directly to the Tower by two men after the crash boat landed her at Portsmouth.

The men were dressed in civilian clothing and looked surprised when they picked her up. They put her in the back seat of a big Daimler car with the curtains drawn and drove her without a stop to London and the Tower. The drive had taken more than two hours, but during that time neither of the men had said anything to her and she had eventually fallen asleep from fatigue. When she woke up, it was to be hurried along through a big door and some narrow corridors to the apartment she was in now.

The next day a gentleman with silver-white hair and a very red face came to see her. He was dressed in a blue uniform with a lot of stripes on the cuffs and had a great many ribbons on his chest.

135

Mrs. Searwood thought vaguely that he was some kind of functionary of the Church Army.

"I'm Air Marshal Noble," he said, "and you I understand are Mrs. Searwood."

"Not any relation of the Nobles of Lower Osbourne, are you?" Mrs. Searwood asked. "One of them was a parson if I remember rightly—Low Church."

"No," said the air marshal. "I am not any relation of the Nobles of Lower Osbourne, madam. And this uniform is that of the supreme commander of the Royal Air Force."

"Uniforms are so confusing," said Mrs. Searwood. "They're supposed to make it easy to recognize the sort of work people do, I suppose. But they make them all look alike."

"Very true, madam," said the air marshal. "However I did not come here to discuss uniforms. I came to find out why you stole one of His Majesty's airplanes and flew it on some wild excursion that ended with your wrecking it in the Channel."

"I did nothing of the sort," retorted Mrs. Searwood.

"You mean you didn't steal the plane?"

"I certainly did not. I borrowed it. And I didn't wreck it. It was wrecked by a German who shot at me. There was something the matter with it. The clocks were all broken and it wouldn't fly any more. But you can't blame me for that. You'd better blame the German. And you can't blame him very well, because I shot him down."

"You what?" cried the air marshal.

"I shot him down," said Mrs. Searwood. "I didn't really mean to, but I was firing the gun and the plane was upside down and he got in the way. I do hope he didn't get hurt because I don't think he'd have shot at me if he'd known it was me and not another young man like himself."

Air Marshal Noble opened his mouth, shut it again and swallowed hard. It was a little while before he could steady himself enough to speak.

"You expect me to believe that you met with a member of the Nazi Luftwaffe, engaged him in aerial combat and shot him down?" he asked. "Balderdash, madam. Balderdash."

"Well, if you can't believe it, don't bother trying because it really doesn't matter." Mrs. Searwood said, "I always think it's best to forget about things you can't believe because then you don't get confused. That's what I did when my husband tried to explain the theory of relativity to me—I just forgot about it."

Air Marshal Noble looked like a man who was suffocating. He opened his mouth ineffectually several times. He ran his finger around the inside of his immaculate white collar, put his hands on the arms of his chair as if to get up, and then slumped back in the seat.

"Madam," he said at length, "I cannot forget it, though I would very much like to, believe me. You stole one of His Majesty's planes—a special plane loaned by the American command, on which experiments were being performed—and you wrecked it. That is a very serious offense indeed, especially in time of war. Now let us start calmly at the beginning. I want you to answer me quite truthfully. Now why did you steal the plane?"

"It's very simple," said Mrs. Searwood. "I wanted to go to France to get some pictures."

"You wanted to go to France to get some pictures," echoed Air Marshal Noble. He said it as if he were in a trance; as if the words had no meaning at all for him; as if they were mere sounds that came out of his mouth without the slightest significance.

"Mrs. Searwood," he thundered, his face purpling, "don't you think you could have waited until the war was over?"

"Oh no!" replied Mrs. Searwood complacently. "You don't understand. The pictures I wanted to get have to do with the war. They were pictures of a new weapon that the Germans have invented to blow up all the people in England. They tried the first one out by aiming it at Lower Pupton where I was living. They've got me down on their black list because I said the Germans were dirty people. That was in Berlin before the war, and a man wrote it down in a little book. Anyway, they didn't hit me because I had just been holding a séance and . . ."

Air Marshal Noble cut her off desperately by waving his hands. "One thing at a time," he said. "One thing at a time. You say there is a new weapon the Germans have invented. How did you know there was a new weapon?"

"Well," said Mrs. Searwood dubiously, "I'll try to explain but I don't think you'll understand. It's a matter of calculation based on the parabola described by Tanner—he's the proprietor of the Fox and Hounds in Lower Pupton—from his bathtub into Mrs. Green's victory garden. People thought it was an earthquake at first, and then they blamed me. Especially Mrs. Manners. But I happen to know it was a rocket."

"Madam," said Air Marshal Noble solemnly, "either one or the other of us is mad. I propose to find out which. Now, we'll start again. About the airplane. You don't deny that you took an airplane?"

"Not at all," replied Mrs. Searwood.

"Well, that's something," said the Air Marshal. "How did you know how to fly it?"

"They're not very hard to fly really," Mrs. Searwood parried. "Not really as hard as driving a car."

"Can you drive a car, madam?"

"Well—I've never tried, so I don't know."

"Have you ever flown an airplane before?"

"No."

"Have you ever studied about flying in books?"

"No."

"Well, how do you account for the fact that you apparently got into a modern fast reconnaissance plane and flew it to France, as you say, without any trouble?" He had a sudden flash of inspiration. "Was there anyone else with you?" he asked. He had hardly posed the question before he realized that it was ridiculous, because there wasn't room in a Mustang for more than one person. To his surprise, however, Mrs. Searwood replied "Yes."

"There was?" said the air marshal. He had a sneaking suspicion that Mrs. Searwood was pulling his leg. "Very interesting indeed. And who, pray, was this remarkably thin person who could fit into the cockpit of a Mustang fighter with you?"

"A Red Indian," replied Mrs. Searwood.

The air marshal emitted a roar like a wounded bear. "Downright blithering nonsense," he cried. "A Red Indian. Where in the whole of England would you find a Red Indian as thin as a needle who can fly an airplane? Answer me that?"

"Well, I did find one," snapped Mrs. Searwood, who decided she'd had enough of this kind of questioning. "And he could fly an airplane. As a matter of fact he can fly any kind of airplane some of which he hasn't invented yet. But it wasn't a Red Indian like you think of a Red Indian. It wasn't a living Red Indian. It was a dead one."

Air Marshal Noble's brick-red face again took on a purplish tinge. Two veins appeared on the sides of his forehead. He opened his mouth gasping like a fish but he couldn't get anything out. He got up from his chair, picked up his briefcase and strode to the door, snorting. As he was about to close it behind him Mrs. Searwood called out, "I know it's hard to believe but you'll find everything I say is true if you look at the film that Ronnie Briggs took. He was in another plane and he got pictures of the rocket."

Air Marshal Noble halted.

"Did you say Briggs?" he asked. He recalled a routine report on a pilot named Briggs arrested on a charge of failure to carry out orders. The man had told some kind of cock-and-bull story, he didn't recall the details, and had been turned over for examination by a psychiatrist.

"Yes," said Mrs. Searwood. "Ronnie Briggs. He knows all about it. Only he didn't see the Indian."

That was too much. Air Marshal Noble snorted and slammed the door behind him.

"Your next caller," said Chief White Feather, "is liable to be a psychiatrist. I'd better give you a good briefing on how to handle him. I don't think you made the right impression on the air marshal."

CHAPTER SIXTEEN

CHRISTINE ADAMS DECIDED that she just had to duck work and go and see Parson Pendlebury right away. She had hardly got a wink of sleep that night and she just had to talk to somebody. There wasn't a bus until midday, so she borrowed a bicycle, got down to the office of the grain merchant where she worked early and left a note for her employer. It said: "I've got to go to Lower Pupton to see the parson. I'll be back soon." Her employer, Mr. Leathers, a man who had lived so long with sacks of grain and cattle cake that he had begun to bear a certain resemblance to his merchandise, read this through twice and scratched his head.

"Someone's dead or someone's going to be wedded," he said. Those were the only two reasons he knew for anyone going to see a parson.

Christine covered the five miles from Winchester to Lower Pupton in half an hour, steamed up the gravel drive to the parsonage, stopped her bicycle by hitting a tub of geraniums and swept into the house.

"Parson Pendlebury!" she shouted, "Mr. Pendlebury. Something dreadful's happened."

"What is it my dear?" asked Mrs. Skipton. "I sent the parson outside while I tidied up. He's probably practicing cricket in the rose garden."

"I've got to see him right away," said Christine, and ran through the living room and kitchen to the garden where she found Mr. Pendlebury, a stout Malacca cane held firmly in both hands, cutting imaginary cricket balls to an imaginary boundary.

140

"Why, Christine," he said, "how nice of you to call. But why aren't you at work?"

"It's Ronnie," said Christine. "They've put him in the poky and they say he's out of his mind. He is not out of his mind. We're going to be married though he hasn't proposed yet and I want you to get him out of the poky."

"There, there, my dear," said the parson, "come and sit down and tell me all about it."

"Well," said Christine, "Ronnie was to see me last night and when he didn't turn up I called up Farnborough. I thought he was standing me up. You know he stayed away from me for a whole month, the beast, just to find out how he felt. I thought he was trying to find out how he felt again and I was going to tell him. But the people at the airfield shuffled me all over the place and eventually a man who said he was a wing commander said that Ronnie was unavailable. I thought perhaps he'd gone out on some mission or other. You know how secret they are about saying anything. So I asked whether I would be able to see him tomorrow or whether he had left any message. And this wing-commander person said he didn't think I would be able to see him for some time and then rang off.

"That really upset me so I called up Corky Peters—he's Ronnie's friend you know, though he's always trying to date me and tried to get me to go out with him a couple of times when Ronnie was staying away from me to find out how he felt—and Corky said they'd put Ronnie in the poky and I'd be a lot better off if I forgot all about him and how about a date.

"Well, I gave him a piece of my mind and asked how they dared put Ronnie in the poky and Corky said the formal charge was failure to accomplish a mission or something silly. But it's worse than that. He said Ronnie kept talking about Mrs. Searwood flying an airplane and going over to France and taking pictures of something over there. And they've got him in a mental ward under observation. He said they'd given him a big basket to weave and when he kicked a hole in it, they gave him a lot of silly little blocks to play with. And oh, Mr. Pendlebury, what am I going to do?" And she broke into tears.

"Now, now," said Parson Pendlebury, patting her hand and very much disturbed himself, "don't worry my dear. I'm sure it's all some terrible mistake. Mrs. Searwood, did you say? Flying an airplane? Good heavens. I never thought that she was a pilot. This is very mysterious indeed. Very mysterious." He recalled with dismay that two days previously he had driven Mrs. Searwood into Farnborough late in the evening. He had been too much of a gentleman to inquire why she wanted to go there and at such a late hour, and she had volunteered no information. All the scraps of gossip about Mrs. Searwood that had come to him through Mrs. Skipton now flooded back; the ridiculous theory of that Mrs. Manners that she was the wife of Rudolph Hess; the story that she had known in advance that the village was going to be bombed; the outrageous canard that she had obtained her remarkable throwing skill while practicing bomb throwing in some Nazi women's league. And then, more hurtful than anything else, the story that she had taken such a prominent part in the restoration of his beloved St. Cedric's window merely to divert suspicion from herself.

It all added up to something very mysterious about Mrs. Searwood. He couldn't bring himself to believe that she was a spy or a traitor, and any one of the charges against her, taken by themselves, were utterly ridiculous. But this last business of flying an airplane . . .

"My dear," he said to Christine with sudden decision, "we'll go right over to Farnborough and see what we can find out. Perhaps they will let me talk to Ronnie since he has come to Lower Pupton and I have known the boy since the day he was born."

They got into the parson's old Morris and chugged off for the airfield.

Mrs. Skipton wasn't by nature a gossip and hadn't really intended to listen. She tried to convince herself that all she had done was take the carpets out on the lawn to beat because they needed beating and had accidentally overheard what Christine was telling Mr. Pendlebury. She hadn't caught the whole conversation because she had had to thump the carpets. If she didn't thump the carpets, that would have been just plain eavesdropping. But in between whacks she had heard Christine say that Ronnie Briggs was out of his mind and in jail and that Mrs. Searwood had been flying an airplane over at the air station at Farnborough. It was just too much to keep to herself, and after the parson had gone she flew through the remainder of the housework, grabbed her bonnet and rushed right down to tell Mrs. Manners.

Mrs. Manners received the information triumphantly. She had been rankling under the stricture placed on her by the corporal sent by Major de Saster telling her not to say anything further about her theories concerning Mrs. Searwood. She suspected that she had not been believed. But here was proof positive that all she had said was true.

"I can't believe that Mrs. Searwood would fly an airplane," said Mrs. Skipton.

"Well, I can," said Mrs. Manners smugly. "I told you that she is really Rudolph Hess's wife and came over here with him and that she learned to fly an airplane in the same women's league of the Nazis where she learned how to throw things. They teach their women everything, my dear. And it's my belief that after blowing up the Fox and Hounds and probably planting bombs all over the place, Hitler had forgiven her and told her she could return to Germany. So she stole an airplane to fly back again, just as Hess stole an airplane in the beginning to fly to England."

This was still too much for Mrs. Skipton and she was sorry now that she had said anything to Mrs. Manners about it. She tried to blow the whole thing down and say that perhaps she hadn't heard Christine right, for she had been beating the carpets at the time. But Mrs. Manners would not be deprived so readily of the justification of all her theories and told the whole story to Mrs. Wedge who dropped in for some groceries. Soon, the whole of Lower Pupton was buzzing with the news that Ronnie Briggs had helped Mrs. Searwood to escape to Germany and had been arrested and was going to be shot the following morning. And that Christine Adams had cycled all the way from Winchester to get Parson Pendlebury to make a last-minute plea to save his life and they had both gone off to Farnborough to see what could be done.

At the Farnborough air station, Parson Pendlebury, after appealing to the chaplain, was permitted to see Ronnie Briggs in the presence of his wing commander. Ronnie was in a room in the mental ward and in a very bad temper. He didn't want to talk to anybody, because he was tired of repeating his story and seeing people glance at each other significantly, but not believing a word.

"It's no use telling anybody about it," he said. "They all think I'm batty and so will you. If they'd just develop the film in my camera they'd find out that every word was gospel. I took pictures of a big rocket in France, and that's all there is to it, and they'll find out if they ever get around to developing my film."

"Is the film being developed?" the parson asked the wing commander.

"Oh, in a routine way," said the latter. "We have to handle an enormous amount of footage here and it will probably take a day or so before we get around to it."

"What about Mrs. Searwood?" the parson asked, somewhat diffidently. Ronnie gave him a calculating look. That was the part of his story where people started looking at each other and nodding their heads sorrowfully.

"What about her?" he parried.

"Well," said the parson, afraid of saying too much, "there's some kind of rumor—no doubt a joke on the part of one of the personnel at the air station—about Mrs. Searwood flying an airplane and you being sent to chase her and bring her down."

"I don't think we have to listen to that kind of nonsense again," cut in the wing commander. "I'm afraid I must ask you to leave now. I'm stretching things a bit by letting you see Briggs at all." He gave Ronnie a curt nod and ushered the parson out of the room. Back in his office he thought a minute and then called the photography section and told them to give priority to the development of the film from the American Mustang.

"Top secret," he continued. "Call me if you find anything worth while on it. Call me anyway."

CHAPTER SEVENTEEN

SIR MURCHISON PROBITT stepped into the Royal Air Force car which had been sent to collect him at his Harley Street office and wondered which one of a host of promising young airmen he was going to have to straighten out now. This had been his work since the outbreak of the war—repairing the delicate minds that controlled the delicate machines whose object was to produce the grossest of destruction. He had volunteered his peculiar talents at the very start of hostilities for this kind of work, and since the mental stress of the conflict in the first instance fell most heavily on the men of the Royal Air Force he had been assigned to that branch and had remained with it, though retaining a restricted private practice.

Sir Murchison, Britain's leading psychiatrist, had gained early fame for himself as a young man by embracing the whole of the Freud doctrine, lock, stock and barrel, at a time when it was regarded as the purest mummery by a conservative British Medical Association.

He had written a number of brilliant papers on the subject, had captured the public imagination with a series of articles in the popular press on the Freudian analysis of such infamous murderers as Dr. Crippen, Mrs. Rouse and Jack the Ripper, and had found a well-paying clientele for his mental medicine among the residents of Mayfair. Then, when British medicine grudgingly moved over to make room for the upstart mental doctors, Sir Murchison had suddenly and dramatically reversed his field.

Freud, he declared, was little more than an intuitive quack. His theory that repressed desires were expressed in distorted dream forms, he maintained, was acceptable in only twenty per cent of cases. Further research, which he had himself conducted, showed that dreams were not always a manifestation of repressed urges or thoughts. The dream itself, he proclaimed, could be the father of the desire instead of vice versa. Dreams could, in short, and often were, the cause of mental unbalance and not merely the symptoms of it, and the way to perfect mental health was to spend a half hour every morning on awaking recalling everything that had been dreamt, and then carefully obliterating all traces of bad dreams, dreams involving evil intentions, from the mind.

This theory, which Sir Murchison called the Neoconscious Motivation of Human Action, had been forcibly demonstrated to him one day while watching his dog asleep. The dog had snapped its jaws together several times during his slumber. When it woke up, although an animal of a gentle disposition, it had bitten the postman—providing, Sir Murchison liked to say, one of the most dramatic demonstrations of cause and effect in the history of modern science. He liked to compare the whole incident to the apple falling on Newton's head.

His theory of Neoconscious Motivation had won for him a knighthood, and Sir Murchison, in his position as psychiatric adviser to the Air Force, had attended almost all members of the cabinet at one time or another with the outstanding exception of the Prime Minister who growled at him that he slept when he liked, dreamed what he wanted to, and thoroughly enjoyed his dreams, good or bad.

Sir Murchison leaned back now in the Air Force limousine as it sped through the drab streets and noted with surprise that he was not being taken to the Air Ministry. Rather the car threaded its way along the embankment to Tower Hill, climbed this short steep incline and then rolled through the double gates of the ancient fortress to stop inside.

"Are you sure we're at the right place?" he asked the driver through the speaking tube before getting out.

"Yes sir," said the chauffeur. "The Tower."

He opened the door smartly and Sir Murchison dismounted with some hesitation. He was sure that there must be some mistake and was about to question the man again when Air Marshal Noble came hurrying towards him.

"Oh, glad you could come Sir Murchison," he said. He seemed to be under a heavy strain. His normally reddish face was rather pale and there were rings of fatigue under his eyes. "A very important matter. Come this way, please." He led him up a flight of stairs to a heavy oak door. Inside they went along a broad, high corridor to an office outside of which a guardsman stood on sentry duty.

"In here," he said and Sir Murchison entered to find himself in a comfortably furnished room in which leather upholstery blended with solid oak. The air marshal waved Sir Murchison to a sofa and sat in a chair behind a desk big enough, almost, for a conference table. He got straight to business.

"Sir Murchison," he said, "I've called on you to ask your help in analyzing a certain woman we have under custody at the present time. This is a highly confidential matter and I know that that is all I have to say to you to ensure that it goes no further. A word to the press and I don't think that even wartime censorship could prevent publicity of the greatest damage to the whole service. Morale would be completely jeopardized."

He paused to let the gravity of the situation sink in.

"What I want you to do is to interview this woman, a rather remarkable woman, and see what you can get out of her. Her name is Martha Searwood, age fifty-four, widowed fifteen years, grown daughter—the whole dossier on her is available. I want you to interview her and decide whether she is sane and whether what she says is to be believed, or whether she is suffering from hallucinations.

"Your decision may affect the whole progress of the war. It may conceivably call for an extensive alteration of second front plans. It may, indeed, spell the difference between life and death for thousands of people in Britain."

Sir Murchison, who had been looking at the floor (it was part of his technique never to look anybody in the eye because he maintained that this constituted a challenge and put them on their guard, making them involuntarily conceal things which they would otherwise say), was so startled that he raised his head and, in violation of his own rules, looked directly at the air marshal.

"I mean every word I am saying," continued the latter. "This is a matter so grave that it is impossible to overstate the case. It demands the utmost secrecy."

"I understand," said Sir Murchison.

"Here, briefly, is the situation. Recently an armed reconnaissance plane was stolen from our airfield at Farnborough. The theft in itself was extraordinary enough, but the circumstances are fantastic. The plane was apparently stolen by this same Mrs. Searwood—a woman, mark you, of fifty-four, who hasn't even got sufficient mechanical experience to drive an automobile.

"Not to go into too much unnecessary detail, the woman admits she had an accomplice. This accomplice," continued the air marshal slowly, "appears to have been a Red Indian who died some three hundred years ago, and is the hottest pilot on either side of the Atlantic."

"I'm not sure that I heard you correctly," said Sir Murchison. "Did you say that this woman's accomplice was a Red Indian who died three hundred years ago?"

"Precisely," said the air marshal. "He also graduated two hundred and seventy-five times from Oxford and Cambridge Universities and was present at the Battle of Waterloo."

"Good heavens," said Sir Murchison. "Tell me, does she think she was also at the Battle of Waterloo?"

"I asked her that," said the air marshal, "and she asked me whether I was out of my mind."

Sir Murchison looked at him narrowly. "You say that this woman took this plane and flew it with the help of an Indian who has been dead three hundred years?" he inquired.

"Certainly," said Noble. "You don't think she could fly it herself, do you? Why we gave her a simple test operating a hand water pump and she was so frustrated by the problem that she threw a fit. I myself, though I have been flying for over thirty years, am not sufficiently familiar with the controls of this particular kind of plane to be able to climb into the cockpit and take off. It must have been an Indian. What am I saying?"

"Tell me," said Sir Murchison quietly, "have you been having any strange dreams lately?"

The air marshal was not acquainted with Sir Murchison's methods and was somewhat shocked by the question. He considered and then said, "Well, for the past two nights, I've dreamt of whole tribes of American Indians stealing every plane we have in Britain and flying them across the Channel."

Sir Murchison plucked his lower lip and shook his head slowly from side to side. "Poor chap," he said. "Poor chap. Too much strain for one man." He considered for a minute and decided to humor him.

"All right," he said, "let's go and see Mrs. Searwood."

CHAPTER EIGHTEEN

MRS. SEARWOOD WAS, for the first time since the start of her adventure, beginning to feel anxious about its outcome. She had been in the Tower for four days and she could not understand why she was being detained so long.

"Surely they must have looked at the picture of the rocket that Ronnie Briggs took by now," she complained to Chief White Feather. "I just can't conceive why they are keeping me so long. You don't suppose that Ronnie went off to see his girl in Winchester instead of reporting back immediately to the airfield? I understand that he always was an irresponsible sort of boy."

"No," said Chief White Feather, "I don't think that's it. But there's something wrong and I'd better try to find out what it is. Probably just official stalling, though something might be wrong with the film Briggs exposed. It's extraordinary the number of people who can't operate such a simple device as a camera. Give them something slightly more complicated than a box Brownie and their whole mental processes fall to pieces. The trouble is that I don't like to leave you here alone to deal with the psychiatrist they're bound to send to question you. It's absolutely vital that you convince him that you're of sound mind. Do you think you know now how to deal with him?"

Chief White Feather had given Mrs. Searwood a lightning course in both psychiatry and psychology from his own studies covering a period of several centuries plus what he'd picked up at Oxford. Mrs. Searwood had been rather bored by it all. She felt that he had added nothing to what she knew already of human nature and marveled that people could have obtained a name for themselves for merely stating things that any woman must learn in the course of dealing with a husband and raising a family.

"Don't bother about me," she said. "I'll give as good as I get. You flit along and find out what happened to the Briggs boy and come right back. I don't want to deal with that Noble man again— I'm not sure that he's in his right mind. I want to see the Prime Minister. I know he's sane. He's not like all these others who every time they take a drink wonder if they're becoming alcoholics."

Chief White Feather left after a little more discussion and he had hardly gone before Air Marshal Noble and Sir Murchison were ushered into her quarters.

"Good afternoon, Mrs. Searwood," said the air marshal. "I've brought along a friend of mine who is interested in your case and he'd like to have a talk with you."

"Interested in my case fiddledeedee," Mrs. Searwood said impatiently. "You've come to find out whether I'm crazy because I said an Indian flew me across the Channel to get some pictures of a German rocket. Well, I'm not."

"Oh no," said Sir Murchison deprecatingly, "not crazy, Mrs. Searwood. As a psychiatrist, I refuse to believe that anybody is ever crazy."

"Then you must be a little touched yourself," Mrs. Searwood retorted, not a whit mollified, "because lots of them are."

Sir Murchison opened his mouth, closed it again and sat down. His mind, after this riposte, had gone blank and he needed a minute or two to think of what it was he wanted to say. He looked at the carpet—his standby in all mental crises—and gradually little trickles of thought came back to him. He decided to start with the Indian.

"All right, Mrs. Searwood," he said, "let us be quite frank with each other. You say that there is an Indian who flies airplanes and who took you off on your rather remarkable expedition. I understand that the Indian has been dead for some time and what you are referring to is the ghost of an Indian. Is that so?"

"He doesn't like to be called a ghost," said Mrs. Searwood. "His name is Chief White Feather and he prefers me to call him a spirit. Ghosts, he says, are rather vulgar."

"A spirit then," said Sir Murchison. "Is he here now, by the way?"

"No," replied Mrs. Searwood. "He went off to find out what happened to Ronnie Briggs and the pictures he took of the rocket."

"Ronnie Briggs?" asked Sir Murchison who was rapidly getting out of his depth.

Mrs. Searwood explained that Ronnie Briggs had accompanied her on the mission in another plane and as she explained about it a look between incredulity and revelation came over Air Marshal Noble's face. When she had finished, he excused himself rather abruptly, saying he would be back in a while but had just remembered some important business he had to attend to right away.

When he had left, Mrs. Searwood asked, "Do you think he's all right?"

"Of course he's all right," said Sir Murchison repentant now at having previously suspected the air marshal of cracking under the strain of his position.

"Well, I'd have thought he was a pound light up here," said Mrs. Searwood, and tapped the side of her head.

"One of the soundest men in England," said Sir Murchison. "Now. To get back to this Indian. You say you have actually seen him?"

"Yes."

"In the daytime?"

"Yes."

"And at nighttime?"

"Yes."

"Have you seen any other gh— I mean spirits?"

"Oh yes," said Mrs. Searwood. "Old Grady, poor thing. He hanged himself after spending all his money on wine and song. He couldn't find any women."

Sir Murchison nodded wisely. The pattern was beginning to take shape. Simple really. A lonely woman who according to her record had had no male companion for fifteen years. Lived alone since her husband died with occasional visits from a rather domineering daughter. Dreamed of the companionship of masculine and protective men as a result of very natural instincts. The dreams, not cleared from her mind when she awakened, had triggered the desire for such companionship. A natural old-fashioned shyness had probably prevented her from seeking out the companionship of living men and so the desire had had to content itself with hallucinations in the form of ghosts. But ghosts were too ordinary—the sort of thing that a lower class of people were impressed by. And so her ghosts were all called spirits. Elementary once you had the training to diagnose the case. He felt a glow of self-esteem as the pattern formed quite clearly for him.

Nothing to do really, he decided, but recommend that she be placed in an institution. Meanwhile he'd ask a few more questions which would illustrate his conclusions and make the case look better when presented as a written report.

"Have you had any vivid dreams lately?" he asked.

"No," said Mrs. Searwood, "I can't remember the last time I had a dream, but it must have been at least thirty years ago. When I go to bed, I just fall asleep and don't know a thing until I wake up in the morning."

"No dreams at all—are you quite sure?"

"Quite sure," said Mrs. Searwood. "Sometimes I wish I had. It seems such a waste all that time sleeping without anything exciting happening. Why do you ask?"

Sir Murchison briefly explained his theory of Neoconscious Motivation, but he didn't explain it as a theory but as fact. Mrs. Searwood listened intently.

"You don't believe in spirits, do you?" she asked quietly.

Sir Murchison said he had to confess that he didn't.

"Do you really think," asked Mrs. Searwood, "that dreams cause people to do things?"

"Not a vestige of a doubt about it," said Sir Murchison.

"But dreams aren't real, are they? I mean, you can't say to someone, 'Look at my dream.' You can't touch them, or bring them out for someone to see, can you?"

"Noooo," said Sir Murchison, "but it's not true, on the other hand, to say that they are not real. They are not *material* is a better way of putting it. They are not like a table or a building or something that you can see and touch and others can see and touch and even enter. They are peculiar in that they are phenomena which, while universal, are at the same time exclusive to the individual." He was feeling in an expansive mood now. He liked to talk about his favorite subject and plunged on.

"On the other hand, dreams are real—very real indeed. They are capable of producing the greatest good or the greatest harm, for they are the fountain from which the human mind draws its desires and ambitions. The ancients were quite right in the high regard in which they held dreams and more sensible in their employment of soothsayers and others to interpret them than are we, who will summon a doctor to mend a broken leg, but never a psychiatrist to explain the significance of a dream, which, unless properly handled, may prove far more dangerous in the long run than broken bones. The curse of our times is that, unlike the ancients, we are too much preoccupied with material things—with what we can touch or taste or see or smell or hear—and have no time for those purely mental phenomena such as dreams which are vastly more important."

"Do you know," said Mrs. Searwood, "I believe every word you say." Sir Murchison smiled benignly. Not an acute case, he thought. Readily susceptible to treatment once he had got her to admit that she had had dreams. He might even take her under his own care. When the secrecy surrounding the matter was removed, it would redound vastly to his credit to have had such a remarkable case and have effected such a remarkable cure.

"Like all great truths," he said, "it is the essence of simplicity."

"Quite so," said Mrs. Searwood, "but I think you have ignored one very important aspect."

"What is that?" asked Sir Murchison good-humoredly.

"Everything you have shown to be true about dreams is true about spirits too," Mrs. Searwood replied.

Sir Murchison was startled. "Ridiculous!" he expostulated. "Why, although many people claim to have seen spirits, no two people have ever been shown to have seen the same spirit at the same time. The thing lacks the very essentials needed for proof."

"And that is true of dreams," said Mrs. Searwood sweetly. "No two people have ever had the same dream at the same time. And even if they had, they couldn't prove it. As I said, everything you hold to be true about dreams is true about spirits. I think your theory is correct, but that you are confusing the two. You think that spirits are merely hallucinations or daydreams. But in reality, dreams and hallucinations are merely spirits . . ."

Sir Murchison started to interrupt but Mrs. Searwood would not let him.

"Let me substitute the word spirit for dream in your exposition and see how we come out," she said. "Let's see. You said that dreams (or spirits) are not material; that they are not like tables and chairs and so on in that you cannot touch them. But that on the other hand dreams (or spirits) are real in that they are phenomena which while universal are exclusive to the individual—that's what you said, wasn't it?"

Sir Murchison had to agree that it was. He wanted to cut off this line of argument for he was beginning to feel uneasy about it, but Mrs. Searwood went on.

"You said too that dreams (and I say spirits) are capable of producing the greatest good or the greatest harm, for they are the fountain from which the human mind draws its desires and ambitions . . ."

"Just a minute," interrupted Sir Murchison, spotting a flaw and grateful for it. "That is certainly true of dreams. They are the mainspring of human ideas and action. But even if I were to admit the existence of spirits, which I do not for an instant, I still would never agree that they can influence human ideas. That is altogether ridiculous."

"Oh no it's not," retorted Mrs. Searwood. "Where do you think people get completely new ideas from? Things that they've never thought of before. Do you think they get them out of thin air—out of nothing? That's silly. Inspiration, which is something, can't come out of nothing, because it's against all sense for something to come from nothing. Inspiration and new ideas you say come from dreams. But I say they come from good spirits. Spirits are around us all the time, and they know the problems we face and can help us to solve them. After all, they've lots more experience than we have. Why, some of them must have been around the world for a million years or more. That would make them very knowing indeed."

"Preposterous!" snorted Sir Murchison. "What about the first men on earth—cave dwellers and so on right at the dawn of time when, I presume, according to your theory, there must have been very few spirits, and those there were were not much better informed than the human beings. What about those first human beings? Where did they get their ideas and inspiration from?"

"They didn't have any ideas and they didn't have any inspiration," replied Mrs. Searwood complacently. "That just proves my point. Why, it took them thousands of years to invent something as simple as a wheel."

Sir Murchison ran his hand over his face as if it were enmeshed in cobwebs and stood up. "This is utter nonsense," he stated with some heat. "Do you expect me to believe that there are spirits all around the place following people about and whispering in their ear every now and then to give them inspiration?"

"Well," said Mrs. Searwood, "I don't know whether you believe it or not, but millions and millions of people do."

"They do not," said Sir Murchison emphatically.

"Oh yes they do," continued Mrs. Searwood, "only they don't call them spirits. They call them guardian angels. They think of them as having wings and being dressed in white robes and keeping a record of everything they do, telling them what is good and advising them against what is evil. It so happens that my guardian angel doesn't have wings and a white robe. He's much more probable. He is a Red Indian and doesn't wear much of anything at all."

Sir Murchison sat down again. He was completely without words and without argument to answer her. He needed to start all over once more. He had never been challenged like this before and the experience was upsetting in the extreme. He looked once more at the carpet to quiet his mind and collect his thoughts. "Mrs. Searwood," he said, like a judge pronouncing sentence, "it is my professional opinion that you are suffering from an acute form of hallucination. The matter is quite clear to me and I do not choose to argue it with you any further."

Mrs. Searwood's heart sank. She had hoped to be able to convince Sir Murchison; indeed she thought for a while that she had. But apparently she hadn't budged him even a little. She had now only one thing more to say.

"Well," she said, "if you think I was suffering from hallucinations, do you think that it was the result of a hallucination that I was able to fly an airplane?"

"Madam," replied Sir Murchison, "I do not believe that you did fly an airplane. I believe that that is all part of the hallucination."

"But what about the nice Navy man who picked me up at sea? He saw me in the airplane, so he knows I was flying it."

"I intend to have a word with him—if indeed he can be found," Sir Murchison said. "People in his mental state should not be holding . . ."

He was interrupted by the return of Air Marshal Noble. He was in a highly agitated state. He looked hard at Mrs. Searwood and then at Sir Murchison and then turned and set the safety lock on the door.

"Briggs," he said to himself and half to them, "Flight Sergeant Briggs."

"What about Briggs?" asked Sir Murchison.

"Everybody has gone out of their minds," replied the air marshal. "I'm mad, you're mad, she's mad and Briggs is mad. Furthermore, so is the commanding officer at Farnborough and the intelligence officer and probably the whole Royal Air Force. I'm washing my hands of this completely. I intend to turn the whole matter over to the Prime Minister."

"What is all this about?" demanded Sir Murchison. "Calm yourself. What is the trouble?"

"Flight Sergeant Briggs," said the air marshal, "who is under arrest at Farnborough for failure to carry out his orders, insists that the plane he was sent to force down or shoot down was piloted by an elderly lady whom he identifies as Mrs. Searwood." He pointed to her dramatically. "Furthermore," he continued, "he insists that Mrs. Searwood persuaded him to accompany her on a mission to France. And he insists that on that mission they not only engaged and shot down three German planes between them, but took pictures of a secret German weapon hidden in a French forest."

He was silent for a minute and then went on in a wooden tone, "And the commanding officer at Farnborough and his intelligence officer insist that in the camera of Briggs's plane they found pictures of a Mustang being flown by an elderly woman who answers to Mrs. Searwood's description, and pictures also of a forty-foot rocket hidden in a forest. There is also a shot of this elderly woman in a Mustang shooting down a Messerschmitt fighter plane—a shot which the commanding officer at Farnborough told me personally over the telephone is a corker."

Mrs. Searwood gave a little sniff of satisfaction.

"I've been telling you that all along but you wouldn't believe me," she said. "I don't know what's the matter with you people. You can't tell the difference between reality and hallucination. You just live in a dream world."

Sir Murchison gave her a shocked and startled look, but he didn't say anything.

CHAPTER NINETEEN

"This," said the Prime Minister, "is the most remarkable assault at arms in the long and stirring history of human warfare. I will not say that it challenges the imagination but rather that it acts as a stimulant and indeed a goad to it. A lone sortie by an elderly Englishwoman, clad in the modern armor of the air, into the very heart of the enemy fortress may well stand beside the deeds of that tender warrior of a prostrate France, Joan of Arc."

He looked at Mrs. Searwood, seated in a leather chair in his office at 10 Downing Street, and realized that perhaps the comparison with Joan of Arc was stretching it a bit. Mrs. Searwood, though dressed in her best, looked tired and a little worn and much too domestic to be heroic. If he were not a man of great heart and great faith and courage, he would not have been able to credit that this somewhat dumpy little woman before him had flown into the European bastion in a Mustang reconnaissance plane, shot down two German aircraft, and secured pictures of the V-2 rocket which might so easily have jeopardized the invasion plans.

"Madam," he said, "your King and his people, and indeed the whole great fellowship of the free peoples of the world, owe you a debt which will weigh heavily upon me as His Majesty's first minister, in that it can never be publicly acknowledged."

He paused to frown at the end of his cigar, groping not for words, for he never failed of them, but to sift and channel his emotions so that on this private and unique occasion, he could adequately sum up and pay tribute to the situation.

160

It could never again be referred to. Indeed, such rumors of the matter as had leaked out must be mercilessly and efficiently eradicated. Once she had left the room, the incident would have to be closed for all time. There could be no record of it, no allusion to it in the future, direct or indirect.

He reflected on the number of people since the beginning of the war who had undertaken missions in a like category—work which by its very nature could never be publicly acknowledged. There were a number of them, and most of them were dead, and had died deaths in circumstances which reeked of treachery but which, if the truth could be told, were deaths of the highest honor and patriotism. But these had all accepted their assignments, fully aware of the hazards involved. Mrs. Searwood had created an assignment for herself and had executed it brilliantly. It had been eminently successful. Already both the United States and Royal Air Force were probing out the launching sites of the V-2 rockets, bombing and harrying them, and although some of the missiles were still reaching their targets in Britain, they were nothing like the number which could have been expected but for Mrs. Searwood.

He was still not quite clear on why she had undertaken the mission. He knew about the rocket that had landed in Lower Pupton—he had known about it within two hours of the explosion. But he didn't understand why this woman had taken it upon herself to trace the missile down to its source at such personal risk.

"I should like to know, madam," he said, "why it was that you felt yourself called upon to undertake this enterprise in the first instance. Do not misunderstand me. I am perfectly aware that you saw in this new weapon a threat to the lives of thousands of your countrymen. I know that it was your intention to thwart this threat. But it seems to me that such vigorous unilateral action on your part must have sprung from some perhaps personal feeling in the matter. Was any relative of yours or perhaps a friend killed by the rocket explosion in Lower Pupton? I do not recall any casualties in the report of the explosion."

"No," said Mrs. Searwood. "It blew Mr. Tanner out of his bath, but I hardly knew him. People thought I had something to do with it because of the séance— I told you about that. That was a good deal of the reason. But it wasn't all. You see the Germans have been after me ever since the beginning of the war."

The Prime Minister gave her a look of mild surprise.

"I venture to suggest," he said, "that they have been after us all."

"I know that," said Mrs. Searwood, "but they took an especial dislike to me. It's all because when I was in Berlin in 1935 having tea at the Adlon and the tablecloth was a little soiled. My teacup wasn't very clean either—I could distinctly see a stain at the bottom of it. Well, I said to my companion that I thought the Germans were a very dirty people. I said it out loud because they were all speaking German and I didn't think they could understand English since they were all foreigners. But one of them did. He was sitting at a table near mine and I saw him write something down in a little book. After that he spoke to the waiter and the waiter brought me a clean cup, but he seemed very annoyed about it.

"Well, after the war started, I knew I was in for it. On the very first bombing raid they hit my apartment. And then they tried to shoot me in broad daylight in Kensington High Street. And before that I'd sent my furniture to a warehouse in Brighton and it had only just been stored there when the warehouse was bombed. And then when I moved to Lower Pupton the very first of those rocket bombs that they sent off was aimed there, though I don't know why they thought I would have been in the Fox and Hounds. I don't frequent public houses . . .

"So you see, I had to find out about it. It was a personal challenge."

The Prime Minister coughed over his cigar. "Precisely, madam," he said.

"There was something more than that too," continued Mrs. Searwood. "Everybody in Lower Pupton got the idea that it was I who blew up the Fox and Hounds. It was that Mrs. Manners. She said I was the wife of Rudolph Hess and had come over with him, and couldn't go back to Germany unless I'd blown up lots of places all over the country. And we were all working together so nicely to get St. Cedric's window restored in the church and then the work stopped because everybody thought I was a pro-Nazi and they didn't want to be associated with me. I don't think the window will ever be finished unless my name is cleared in the village. Even Parson Pendlebury isn't quite sure about me though he would never say a word against me, the dear man."

There was a silence while the Prime Minister tried to absorb this last basketful of miscellaneous and, to him, completely unconnected intelligence. He decided to ignore it for the moment.

"I understand," he said, "though Air Marshal Noble was not at all clear on the matter and I have had all the records in the case destroyed as a matter of security—I understand that you were fortunate enough to obtain the services of an accomplice in the piloting of the plane. Can you, under the seal of secrecy, tell me who this was?"

Mrs. Searwood hesitated. This was the point of her story which she had the most difficulty getting anyone to believe.

"I'd rather not," she demurred.

"You may rely entirely on my discretion," said the Prime Minister, with old-fashioned courtesy.

"Oh," said Mrs. Searwood, blushing, "it's nothing like that. It's just that most people don't believe me."

"I am accustomed," said the Prime Minister, "to accepting the incredible as commonplace." He waited.

"Well," said Mrs. Searwood, "if you won't send me to that silly psychiatrist again, I'll tell you. It was an Indian, an American Indian called Chief White Feather. He died nearly three hundred and fifty years ago, so it was his spirit really. He came over to England with an Indian princess called Pocahontas and liked it so much that he stayed here." She was talking rapidly now. "He graduated two hundred and seventy-five times from Oxford and Cambridge, is an expert on everything and knows all about missiles and airplanes and philosophy and so on."

There was a short silence while the Prime Minister drew on his cigar and allowed the smoke to trickle out of his mouth. It was almost as blue as his eyes which were fixed steadily on her, betraying nothing.

"Oxford," he said at length. "I don't say that he was wasting his time there, but he would have done better to have gone to Sandhurst."

"You mean that you believe about the Indian?" Mrs. Searwood asked, pleased and surprised.

"Madam," the Prime Minister replied, "I am not in the habit of doubting the word of a lady. Nor do I feel any present inclination to doubt. There are many matters in life, which defeating as they do the lower processes of the mind, must be accepted on faith. Indeed, I hardly have to remind you that there have been times in our recent history when if reason had not bowed to faith, all would have been lost."

"'On the beaches and in the fields'" said Mrs. Searwood half to herself. "'Until in God's good time . . .'"

"Yes," said the Prime Minister. "That was one such occasion. No, I do not doubt your Indian, madam. Indeed, had the Nazi hordes gained our Channel coasts, I looked for the sounding of Drake's drum and the return of that mighty warrior to fight by our side. You perhaps know the poem:

"Take my drum to England, hang it by the shore,
Strike it when your powder's running low . . ."

They were both silent for a while. Mrs. Searwood was thinking how nice it was to find someone who believed in Chief White Feather and the Prime Minister was thinking back to another war and the legend of the Angels of Mons, who, armed with long bows like the men of Agincourt, had fought beside the machine gunners of a stricken British Army, loosing yard-long shafts of fire. Many soldiers swore by the story, telling of a great light that had descended between the two armies and sent the enemy reeling back. Then there were the voices that had spoken to Joan of Arc. He mused on a while.

"Well," he said at length, "to return to the matter at hand. I am at a disadvantage in that I cannot adequately recompense you for the services you have rendered your King and country. For such signal valor it would be proper to award the title of Dame—equivalent to that of Knight—together with some such decoration as befits the occasion.

"But this may not be done. The bestowing of such an honor, however well merited, would call for explanations and I dread to visualize the effect on the population if it were to be revealed that in—ahem—certain remarkable circumstances it is possible for a woman of mature years to appropriate one of His Majesty's warplanes and fly it wherever she wishes.

"It remains then, only for me to thank you personally and privately for your services to the realm, and to inquire if there is any favor not involving official recognition or announcement, which I can procure for you."

"I would like the people in Lower Pupton, and particularly that Mrs. Manners, to know that I'm not Rudolph Hess's wife and that I didn't blow up the Fox and Hounds. I want to go back there," Mrs. Searwood said.

"I believe that can be arranged," replied the Prime Minister. He picked up the telephone and asked to be connected with Lord Beston, publisher of the *Daily Distress*.

"Beston?" he asked. "A former naval person speaking. I wonder if you could find it convenient in the national interest to publish prominently somewhere in your newspapers a picture of Mrs. Rudolph Hess. Ah, and another thing. I'm requesting the Ministry of Information to give a press conference about the recent explosions which have been taking place in different parts of the country. No sense in maintaining secrecy any longer. We know what they are all about. I'd like you to send one of your more skilled young men to the conference. Yes. There'll be a survivor on hand. A certain Mr. Tanner. He was blown out of his bathtub. Not a word, of course, until the press conference is arranged. Thank'ee."

He put down the receiver and turned to Mrs. Searwood.

"That, I think," he said, "will attend to the situation in Lower Pupton as well as the numerous rumors which have been bruited around the country. Now, is there any further way in which I can be of service to you?"

"Well," said Mrs. Searwood, "there is but I'd rather not mention it."

"A personal matter perhaps?" said the Prime Minister.

"Yes," said Mrs. Searwood. "Do you have a woman secretary on your staff?"

"Certainly," replied the Prime Minister. He pressed a button on his desk and a woman entered—a woman, to Mrs. Searwood's relief, of her own age.

"I could write it down and give it to this lady," said Mrs. Searwood shyly.

"Certainly, madam," said the Prime Minister. He gave her paper and pencil and Mrs. Searwood scribbled a note and gave it to the secretary.

WHEN SHE HAD GONE, the Prime Minister was hard put to contain his curiosity.

"Is this request of Mrs. Searwood's of so private a nature that I must be completely interdicted from knowing of it?" he asked a little petulantly.

"I don't think so," said the secretary. "In fact I'm sure it was just that she didn't want to say it to you personally because it would be embarrassing." She handed Mrs. Searwood's note to him and he read, coloring slightly: "Could I please have a new girdle—size 36?"

CHAPTER TWENTY

Mrs. Searwood returned quietly to Lower Pupton, taking the bus from Winchester as she had done on her first visit. She had been away ten days and in the interim a great many things had happened in the village as indeed had happened to her.

To begin with, her sudden and unexplained disappearance had set all the gossips buzzing, and then the story of her escaping to Germany with the aid of Ronnie Briggs had really produced a sensation. Parson Pendlebury, on his return from Farnborough, had found himself vigorously denying that Ronnie Briggs was going to be shot and that Mrs. Searwood had stolen an airplane from the airfield, and in the end had taken to the pulpit to preach a sermon against the evil of gossip, however innocently indulged in. A meeting of the local Home Guard and its auxiliary had been summoned in the Old Barn and there Ronnie's wing commander had addressed the audience with a few crisp and well-chosen words on the subject of the danger of speculating on the activities of any member of His Majesty's armed forces.

Admiral Gudgeon had rather spoiled the effect by taking the opportunity to give a discourse on the superiority of the naval over all other branches of the service, and the wing commander had somewhat awkwardly had to get the topic back under control with a tribute to Admiral Gudgeon, a few remarks on the reliance of a modern fleet on its aircraft carriers and a pointed discussion of the lengthy training required before it was possible for anyone to fly a modern warplane.

On the following day, Mrs. Manners had been summoned to Winchester for an interview with Major de Saster. She had gone with a certain air of superiority, confident that all she had to say about Mrs. Searwood would be shown to be true. She had returned, however, remarkably subdued and uncommunicative, and Major de Saster's corporal, who had, as a result of his numerous visits to the village struck up an acquaintanceship with Elsie, Mrs. Green's daughter, let it be known that the major had "read her off good and proper."

"Wouldn't like to have been in her shoes," he said. "Had her on the carpet and done her up brown, he did," the corporal told Elsie. "Started with a lecture about careless talk costing lives and then showed her an official photograph of Hess's wife, asked her if it looked like Mrs. Searwood, and then told her that if she wanted to stay out of serious trouble, to say nothing more of Mrs. Searwood, Ronnie Briggs or the Fox and Hounds to anyone."

This had been followed the next day by a front-page story in the *Daily Distress*, of which a liberal distribution took place in Lower Pupton, dealing with the rocket weapon. "HITLER SUPER WEAPON FAILURE," the headlines read. "VILLAGE PUBLICAN UNHURT THOUGH BLOWN FROM BATHTUB. 'THOUGHT IT WAS THE PLUG' HE REPORTS." Next to it was a picture of Mr. Tanner, his hand indomitably holding a beer-pump handle and his streak of hair, not a particle of it disturbed, pasted over his dome.

Lower down in the page was a two-column picture of Mrs. Rudolph Hess with her child. The caption hinted somewhat vaguely that she was reported to be ill through worry over the fate of her husband.

All this served to completely discredit the village's previous theories concerning Mrs. Searwood, and the gossip was finally laid to rest when Ronnie Briggs turned up to report that he had merely been undergoing treatment for athlete's foot. He had been cautioned about saying anything further of his adventures to anyone, told he would be recommended for a Distinguished Flying Cross after a decent interval had elapsed, and given a week's sick leave.

Thus, when Mrs. Searwood returned to Lower Pupton, the village was in a thoroughly repentant mood. Each felt himself especially guilty of a gross lack of charity to a stranger who had come among them, and the news of her arrival had hardly spread around the houses and cottages before they started calling on her.

Mrs. Skipton was first with news of fresh eggs and lamb chops and all the bits of gossip in the village (excluding any reference to Mrs. Searwood) that she could get together as a peace offering.

Mr. Wedge had held a meeting, she said, and almost everyone in the village had attended, and all had agreed to start work again with even greater vigor on the restoration of St. Cedric's window. Admiral Gudgeon had volunteered a donation of twenty pounds to the building fund and Mr. Wedge was putting up a further ten and all together another eighty-five pounds had been subscribed. But they wanted her to act as treasurer and general supervisor of the project. Mrs. Searwood was delighted. Now that she had her new girdle the window was the project dearest to her heart. She had a feeling that if they could get it finished it would be quite as big a thing as winning the war, because, as she explained to Chief White Feather later, if people did things like that, as a community, during a war, it showed that they had really won irrespective of the military outcome.

"I can't recall a saner remark," Chief White Feather replied. "Sometimes you astound me with a kind of instinctive intimacy with the essence of quite deep truths."

"Mrs. Green said the same thing," said Mrs. Searwood. "She said she didn't plant her victory garden to get victory but because the proper thing to do with ground was grow things in it, particularly Brussels sprouts. She likes Brussels sprouts though I can't say I'm fond of them myself."

The next to call was Mrs. Manners. She was a little shamefaced, rather like a sparrow that had been chirping away busily and been caught in a drenching shower of rain. Now that she was over the mortification of her interview with Major de Saster, and in the face of the evidence in the *Daily Distress*, she was truly repentant and Mrs. Searwood felt rather sorry for her.

"We're so glad to see you back," Mrs. Manners said when they were seated together in the living room, "and I really feel very sorry about all the things I said. You know, I just get to thinking and then talking and before I know it I've said all sorts of things that I really don't mean."

"Don't give it another thought my dear," said Mrs. Searwood, too delighted over the news of the window to harbor any ill feelings. "I know just what you mean, and it's all over now. Let's just have a cup of tea and forget it."

"We were all very worried about you going away in such a hurry," continued Mrs. Manners, perking up immediately at her absolution and her active mind questing like a ferret for some further gossip.

"It wasn't really a hurry," said Mrs. Searwood unthinkingly. "I'd been thinking it over for quite some time before I made up my mind." She regretted the statement, which was not quite true, almost immediately and Chief White Feather was quick to chide her.

"Look," he said, "you can't say things like that. You disappear from the village in dead of night with Parson Pendlebury without telling a soul where you're going or giving anyone any notice and then say you've been thinking it over for some time and finally made up your mind. The statement is, to say the least of it, suggestive."

"You just have the wrong kind of mind," said Mrs. Searwood aloud.

Mrs. Manners flushed swiftly for she had been thinking along the suggestive lines to which Chief White Feather alluded. Mrs. Searwood recovered herself and said, "Not you, my dear. It's just my habit of thinking out loud. I wasn't talking to you at all. I suppose I did go away in a hurry, but I had some important business to attend to in London, and just had to leave right then."

Mrs. Manners made a mental note that the parson had said he had driven her to Farnborough, but decided not to comment at this juncture.

"Let's switch this conversation," said Chief White Feather. "You're not only losing ground but reputation as well. Get off the defensive. Ask her some questions."

"How is Parson Pendlebury?" asked Mrs. Searwood.

"Oh Lord," groaned White Feather, "what a question to ask—of all the people you know in this village, the first one you inquire about on your return is Parson Pendlebury."

"He's been worried ever since you went away," Mrs. Manners said breathlessly. "Mrs. Skipton says he hasn't been eating much and goes for walks and then comes back again about five minutes after he sets out. Then he goes out in the garden to practice cricket and before you know it, she says, he's back in the kitchen asking for a newspaper. Mrs. Skipton says she's never seen him acting like that before."

"He must have something on his mind, poor man," said Mrs. Searwood.

"Yes, my dear," said Mrs. Manners archly, "and I don't think it's the text for his Sunday sermon."

When she had gone, Chief White Feather reprimanded Mrs. Searwood for what he said was a most maladroit piece of conversation on her part.

"You're just not used to villages," he scolded, "though I've already warned you about Mrs. Manners. She's just like a broadcasting station. She just has to go on the air at regular intervals with the latest news. There's already a considerable section of the village that believes there's some kind of romantic liaison between you and the parson. If you take my advice you'll go back to London and stay there for a while and give the village a chance to settle down again."

"I like it here," said Mrs. Searwood, "and I'm not going back. It's nice to be the center of attention after having no one to talk to or talking about me all these years. Besides, there's the window. I want to see that complete."

"But think of the parson," said White Feather. "Mrs. Manners, deprived of her original theories concerning you, is bound to stir up something. It's her nature. And if she does it may well affect Pendlebury's position in the parish and he may lose his livelihood, which would be a hard thing at his time of life."

"Parson Pendlebury, I'm sure, can well look after himself," retorted Mrs. Searwood. "He's a man of mature years and with much experience behind him, and I would say, a man well capable of deciding on what course of action to take in any kind of situation."

"But what course of action is there for him to take with Mrs. Manners making all kinds of nonsense about him driving you to Farnborough during the night? He had a flat tire on the way back, you know, and didn't return to the parsonage until some time the following morning. You've already had some experience of what Mrs. Manners can do with the slightest oddity of circumstance. She'll be weaving her romances now, or I miss my guess. And gossip isn't the kind of thing you can deal with directly. The parson can't make an announcement from the pulpit that he has no interest in you beyond friendship. It isn't done, and furthermore he wouldn't be believed. If you stay here, every time the two of you are together, people are going to make a great deal of it. Villagers must gossip, for they haven't got the murders and bank robberies to talk about that divert the townsman, and deprived, as they have been, of one sensation they won't pass up the opportunity for developing another. They'll have you and Pendlebury carrying on a clandestine affair and the whole thing will probably get to the Bishop in the end, magnified several times more, and the parson will be in real trouble. You know clergymen are in a peculiar position. They must not only never do anything that is wrong, they must also live in such a way that no suspicion of misbehavior can be attached to even their most innocent actions.

"Now, just what can the parson do to effectively quell the gossip that is bound to arise concerning his relations with you?"

Mrs. Searwood did not reply immediately. She went over to the mirror and touched a few stray white curls into place with her fingers.

"I'm sure that's not for me to say," she said.

The significance of her answer was lost for a minute on Chief White Feather. When he caught it, he gave her a look of mingled incredulity and admiration.

"So that's how it is," he said and walked through the wall.

CHAPTER TWENTY-ONE

"Listen here," said Christine the next time she was out with Ronnie Briggs, "what's all this rot about having athlete's foot and staying away from me for ten days and refusing to answer the telephone? And then getting that Corky Peters to tell that silly story about Mrs. Searwood flying an airplane and after I'd gone all the way over to Farnborough with Parson Pendlebury filling him full of nonsense about some pictures that had to be developed?

"Were you staying away so as to find out how you felt again?"

"No," said Ronnie nervously, "I wasn't. I know how I feel." He had been dreading this moment knowing full well that Christine was going to put him through a pretty severe inquisition.

"Well," said Christine, "I'm waiting. How do you feel?"

"Fine now," said Ronnie. "They gave me some kind of ointment and wrapped them in bandages."

"Not your feet," said Christine. "You know very well I don't mean that. I mean how do you feel about how you feel?" If he'd have told the truth he'd have said he felt weak and trembling and that there was something in his throat the size of a pipe wrench and he couldn't get it either up or down. He'd have added too that every time he looked at her he felt like the time he got his first brand-new motor bike, all paid for.

But instead he said in a voice that sounded to him as though it belonged to a small boy sitting beside him, "I'm stuck on you. That's how I feel. My clutch has been slipping since the day we met. Will you marry me?"

"Darling," said Christine. "How perfectly wonderful. I'd been planning on it all along." And she threw her arms around his neck.

PARSON PENDLEBURY was suffering from the worst of all mental pains—indecision. He was quite unaccustomed to it, and took it with bad grace. In all his nearly sixty years of life there had never arisen an occasion when he had not been able to marshal the facts, examine each one frankly, add up the pros and cons and come to a decision.

And now he had before him a problem of great importance, and no sooner had he arrived at one decision about it, than it would appear to him that the alternative was the better solution. And when he adopted the alternative, it was to find it not so sound a course after all, and he would go back to the original.

The trouble, he told himself, was that this was a problem affecting not just him but somebody else. He had to work out a solution that not only agreed with his own desires, but was best for her too. And the matter defeated him.

Eventually he took a piece of paper and divided it down the middle with a neat line. At the top of one half he wrote, "Arguments in favor of marrying Mrs. S." (He could not quite bring himself to put her name there.) On the top of the other half he wrote, "Arguments against marrying Mrs. S."

In the "for" column he wrote:

1. Mrs. S. is a cultivated and intelligent woman of my generation.
2. Mrs. S. is, I would judge, lonely.
3. I am lonely.
4. By taking Mrs. S. late at night to Farnborough without explanation and returning much later than I had anticipated I have compromised her position.
5. Village gossips are already putting an unfortunate construction on this and the effect on my parish is not good.

6. It is the part of a gentleman to ask her hand in
   marriage to extract her from an unfortunate situation.
7. I am very fond of Mrs. S.

When he had read it through he underlined the word *very*.
In the "against" column he wrote:

1. Mrs. S. does not know me very well.
2. Marriage is for young people and we are both elderly.

He could think of no more "against" arguments, but decided to
underline item two in that column. For him it seemed to outweigh
all the arguments in the "for" column. There was no denying it. He
had but two years to go to sixty and although he was in good health
a man was old at sixty, or getting old anyway. And marriage, as he
noted, was for young people.

He threw his pen down with a sigh, crumbled the piece of paper
up and put it in his pocket and was about to go into the garden and
seek some comfort from his flowers when there came a knock at
the door and Mrs. Skipton entered.

"Young Briggs would like to see you, sir," she said.

"Briggs?" echoed the parson. "Oh yes, Ronnie Briggs. Show him
in. Ah, how are you Ronnie? You're looking well, very well indeed.
Over all your troubles now, I hope?"

"Yes indeed, Padre," Ronnie said, "it all came out all right in
the end. I wish you'd forget about it though. Sticky kind of thing
while it lasted."

"Don't give it a moment's thought," said the parson. "Nobody's
said anything to me, and I haven't made any more inquiries.
Athlete's foot, I understand, can be quite a disturbing condition,"
and he gave Briggs a quick wink.

"Rather," said Ronnie.

The parson motioned him to a chair and Ronnie sat down and
fumbled for a cigarette. Mr. Pendlebury noticed that his hand

trembled a little as he lit it and this surprised him, for apart from the little episode in the mental ward at Farnborough, he had always known Ronnie to be a young man with practically no nerves at all.

"Something on your mind?" he asked at length.

"Yes," said Ronnie, "nothing much. Well, I suppose it really is, come to think of it. Actually it's frightfully important."

"Fire away," said the parson.

"Well," Ronnie said, "it's about my girl, Christine. We want to get married and we'd like to publish the banns here and in Winchester and have you perform the wedding in your church."

"Splendid," said the parson heartily. "I was hoping that something of the sort would develop. And I'm so glad you decided to be married in Lower Pupton. Congratulations indeed. We must have a drink on that." He went to the sideboard and returned with a decanter containing some port wine and two glasses. They each took a solemn sip.

"Let's see," said Mr. Pendlebury, looking at a calendar on his desk, "it's the end of May. The banns will take us into June so you will have a June bride."

"That's just what she wants," said Ronnie. He seemed uncomfortable. "She wants a real church wedding with bells and flowers and all that, and I haven't been able to talk her out of it."

"A very sensible girl indeed," said the parson. "Marriage is a remarkable sacrament in that it is conferred by the two parties involved, one on the other, and is merely blessed by the church. It has come to be regarded as a civil contract—you have to have a license of course. But it's something much deeper than that. It is a joyful and at the same time solemn acceptance by two people of each other to the exclusion of all others. Bells and flowers are certainly part of it and I think I can arrange for the choir to sing the wedding music if she would like that."

"I'm sure she would," said Ronnie. He hesitated for a while and then continued, "There's only one thing more. Christine is an orphan with no near relatives. As there would be no one to give her away, she wants to feel that she's coming from someone to me—

being given to me—you know how women are. So I suggested that perhaps Mrs. Searwood would act as her sponsor and she was delighted. I had intended to call on Mrs. Searwood at the first opportunity and ask her myself, but she wasn't home when I passed by though she was expected back shortly. I have to get back over to Winchester immediately to see Christine. She carries on terribly if I'm late. I wonder whether you would be good enough to ask Mrs. Searwood for me, Padre. Explain that I did call but she wasn't in and so on. I'm sure she'll understand."

"I'm sure she will," said the parson.

"A remarkable woman," said Ronnie, reflectively.

"A very remarkable woman," said the parson and the two looked at each other each wondering how much the other knew of his reasons for the statement.

PARSON PENDLEBURY called on Mrs. Searwood that evening. When he arrived at the Yews he had the same feeling of mixed anticipation and anxiety he had experienced years ago when making his first call on his bishop.

Mrs. Searwood looked even more refreshing than when he had first met her—it seemed months ago although it was but a matter of weeks. Her feet were trim in a new pair of shoes and she seemed to have had her hair done in some special way that made her face look surprisingly younger. She had on one of those gay prints that she was so fond of, for the evening was sunny and warm and there was the murmuring of bees in the garden and the sound of doves from the trees in the back of the house.

This was the first time he had seen her since her return. He had wanted to call on her right away but thought it would be more seemly to delay a day or two, particularly since he understood from Mrs. Skipton that the whole village had been flocking in and out of the Yews in an almost constant procession, and he knew that in such circumstances he would hardly have a chance of talking to her privately.

"Come right in," Mrs. Searwood said, smiling her welcome. "I've been looking forward to seeing you again to thank you once more

for driving me to Farnborough. It was very kind of you. I understand you had some trouble on the way back. I do hope you weren't too much inconvenienced."

"Think nothing of it," said the parson. "I was only too glad to be of assistance. I trust er—that everything went off well."

"Excellently," said Mrs. Searwood. "Some day perhaps I'll tell you all about it. But not now. Do sit down and make yourself comfortable and I'll make a pot of tea." She went out to the kitchen and the parson went over to the mirror over the mantelpiece and looked at himself anxiously. That beard, he told himself, maybe if I shaved it off. He covered it with his hands and was standing there examining the effect when Mrs. Searwood came back with the tea tray.

"I hope you weren't thinking of cutting off your beard," said Mrs. Searwood. "I find it most distinguished. So many men these days are clean-shaven, as if they are afraid to acknowledge their years."

"Thank you indeed," said Mr. Pendlebury. "I was toying with the idea—just for a change, you know," he added hurriedly.

"Well, don't give it another thought," said Mrs. Searwood. "I will admit that when I first saw it, it gave me a surprise. But I've come to like it now. Indeed, you wouldn't be yourself without it, and people should be what they are."

She poured the tea deftly, not spilling a drop and the parson was so lost in admiration at this that she surprised him looking devotedly at her. He fumbled for something to say to cover his embarrassment and plunged immediately to business.

"You remember Ronnie Briggs, the flier?" he asked.

"Yes indeed. A very nice young man."

"He's just been to see me on a somewhat unique errand."

"Oh." Mrs. Searwood experienced a moment of anxiety. She had not seen Ronnie since the rocket episode and she was afraid that he might have been talking to the parson about it. That would be very hard to explain at the moment. Indeed, it couldn't be explained and would upset everything.

"Yes," continued the parson, "he's going to be married, you know."

Mrs. Searwood sighed with relief and managed to say delightedly, "How nice."

"Yes," answered the parson. "Indeed, it is for that reason that I called to see you. His fiancée, a young lady named Christine Adams—I fancy you met her at the garden party—wants a church wedding in Lower Pupton, and of course I was delighted to tell him that I would be glad to officiate.

"It appears, however, that Miss Adams is an orphan, and so she has no one to give her away. She is very anxious to have a sponsor at her wedding and young Briggs thought of a solution which I'm sure you will find quite a compliment to yourself. He asked me to approach you and inquire whether you would be willing to give the young lady away and I told him I'd be glad indeed to put the matter to you."

"Why, of course," said Mrs. Searwood. "I'd love it. She'll need all sorts of help in getting ready, and I'll be delighted to stand for her. When is the wedding to be?"

"Toward the end of June," replied the parson.

"Oh my, we haven't much time. There's so much to be done. There's the bridesmaids to arrange for and the flowers and the wedding dress and the invitations and a host of things. Perhaps she would like to have her reception here at the Yews. It's so long since I went to a wedding—the last was my daughter's many years ago. How nice of Miss Adams. I'm really very honored. I must arrange to see her immediately. We'll be very busy indeed. A June wedding—and in a church. This takes me back very many years indeed."

"And me," said the parson. "Of course I've officiated at many weddings, but young people these days are in such a hurry, they hardly seem to enjoy a wedding. Everything done on the spur of the moment. You'd be surprised at the number of bride-grooms who turn up without a ring."

"That's true," said Mrs. Searwood, "but of course there can be such a thing as hesitating too long. I don't think the long engagements of our youth were such a good thing. They put a great strain on couples, and I really believe resulted in many weddings being canceled that might have been thoroughly successful if it hadn't been for the artificial delay."

This surprised and encouraged the parson.

"Do you really think that people should make up their minds and then get married as soon as possible afterwards?" he asked.

"Certainly," replied Mrs. Searwood. "Of course, with very young people it's different—some of them really don't know whether they *have* made up their minds. But the Briggs boy is old enough to know what he wants. It's quite silly for people with experience in living, as he has, to subject themselves to a waiting test when they know perfectly well what is good for them."

This was the parson's opening and he knew it. In a second, just a second, he could say what it was he wanted to. But there seemed to be a ledge in the back of his mind; an impediment that he could not get the words over. How terrible, he thought, if she laughed at me; told me we were both too old for such a thing. He hesitated, groping for the words he needed so desperately; words which would convey his fervor and sincerity, and yet would not sound blundering and impetuous. If he could lay tongue to the words, he would say them experimentally to himself, and if they passed judgment, say them out loud. He searched his mind for them, and mechanically put his hand in his pocket for his pipe.

He found the pipe and brought it out, and then realized with a spasm of horror that the piece of paper on which he had written down the pros and cons of this very situation was no longer there. Quickly he fumbled through his other pockets but without result. The all-revealing paper, in his own handwriting, was gone; lying perhaps somewhere around the village or in his own house, for prying eyes to see and wagging tongues to make the most of.

"Is there something wrong?" asked Mrs. Searwood, noting his dismay.

"I've lost something. A rather important piece of paper on which I had put down some—some notes of a personal nature."

"Well, let's look for it," said Mrs. Searwood practically. "If you dropped it here, it won't be very far." They commenced a search of the room. They turned over every cushion and went on their hands and knees to look under the chairs and sofas. They looked behind the door and out in the corridor and in the garden, but not a trace of the incriminating paper could be found.

"Perhaps I left it at home on my desk," said the parson. "I think I ought to go and look right away. Would you excuse me?"

He was so genuinely concerned that Mrs. Searwood made no attempt to detain him, but assured him that if she found the paper she would bring it to him right away.

Back at the vicarage, the parson searched his study without avail. The paper was nowhere to be found.

In desperation he began going through his pockets again, knowing full well that he had searched them thoroughly a dozen times already. And then, miraculously and impossibly, there it was, right in the same pocket of his coat in which he had put it. He opened the twisted and crumpled scrap to assure himself that it was indeed the same paper and was about to tear it up when he saw that in the "against" column something else had been added.

Under Item Two: "Marriage is for young people and we are both elderly," was written in a feminine hand: "Nonsense. Why don't you ask her? She'd probably say yes." He stared at this in disbelief for several seconds, read it over slowly two or three times and eventually read it out loud.

Then he got into his car, neglecting his hat, and drove right back to the Yews to be admitted by a surprised Mrs. Searwood. He did not give her an opportunity to recover.

"Madam," he said, as soon as she had closed the door behind him, "will you marry me?"

"Why, of course," said Mrs. Searwood, as if this was the most natural thing in the world.

CHAPTER TWENTY-TWO

IT WAS A JUNE WEDDING—a June wedding in a war that everyone felt was approaching its climax and its close. The invasion had been launched and things were going almost better than had been expected. The bombing raids had slacked off and people were beginning to make plans, still tentative though no longer quite forlorn, about what they were going to do when peace returned. And added to all this, this particular June had come gloriously full of life, so that everyone said there never had been so many roses.

The church at Lower Pupton was full of them. They were packed into the sanctuary and upon the altar, and festoons of them hung from the choir loft. And there were masses more before the window of St. Cedric now restored to its original beauty. The villagers, still repentant over their gossip about Mrs. Searwood, and spurred on by Mr. Wedge and Admiral Gudgeon who had unexpectedly deserted his naval discourses to lend a hand, had worked night and day to get the window repaired in time for the wedding of their parson and Mrs. Searwood.

The Bishop himself, who was to preside at the wedding, or rather the double wedding, rededicated the window before the start of the ceremony and in a little address complimented the village and particularly the parson and Mrs. Searwood for their work.

"When," he said, "the spirit of a true Christian reverence is so deeply embedded in a people that even in the midst of the distractions and anxieties of war, they have time and inclination to turn

184

to that work which honors their Creator, then there is no need to be troubled about the real health of a community or of a nation."

When the curtain was pulled aside, St. Cedric stood there in all his glory smiling calmly upon them all as if to acknowledge that they were the same people he had known during his own life on earth and whom he had fought to defend.

Then the wedding ceremonies began. First one bride, Mrs. Searwood, gave away the other bride, Christine Adams, who became Mrs. Ronnie Briggs. And then Mrs. Searwood herself stood before the altar and became Mrs. Lawrence Pendlebury, wife of the Rector of Lower Pupton.

The whole village was there, of course, packing the church and overflowing into the pleasant churchyard beyond. The society editor of the *Hampshire Echo* who had come from Winchester, for it was not often that the Bishop officiated at a wedding, interviewed Mrs. Searwood's daughter Priscilla to get a few notes for her story.

Priscilla was somewhat at a loss here. She had been very busy in London and although intending for some time to visit her mother in Lower Pupton, had not been able to manage it.

She had come at last in answer to a rather rambling letter which complained about the need for pumping water by hand at the Yews, about the number of wasps in the pantry, gave elaborate details of the restoration of a window in a church and somewhere towards the end announced that her mother was getting married the next week or so to a Mr. Pendlebury, "who is a very nice man indeed."

That had been enough. Priscilla got the next train to Winchester and the next bus to Lower Pupton, convinced that her mother was in her dotage and had taken up with some conniving man, probably a gamekeeper or some member of the lower classes.

She was surprised to learn that her prospective stepfather was the village rector, had attended public school, played cricket for Hampshire, and for all his quiet manner was remarkably adroit at keeping her in her place. After finding that her mother's mind was made up, she accepted it all as being for the best and plunged into the wedding plans with an efficiency that shook the village.

Of how the romance had developed, of her mother's remarkable experiences in flying a plane, however, she learned nothing. So she had to content herself with telling the society editor of the *Hampshire Echo* that the bride and groom were old friends and leaving it at that.

After the ceremony, both couples went to the rectory, where a reception was given and where Mrs. Searwood changed into her going-away clothes for her honeymoon.

She could not remember when she had felt so happy—not in many many years, and as she seated herself before the mirror, trembling a little with all the excitement, the realization that the end of all her loneliness had come at last, that no more would there be an empty square apartment to go back to in the evening, was so much for her that she had to let the tears come.

When she looked up, she saw Chief White Feather standing behind her, looking a little sad himself.

"You mustn't cry now, my dear," he said gently. "All the troubles are over and there's nothing ahead but happiness."

"That's what I'm crying about," said the new Mrs. Pendlebury. "I can't quite believe it's true. It's like reading it in a book. It is true, isn't it?"

"Just as true as I'm standing here," said Chief White Feather.

"You are standing there, aren't you? You seem to be getting paler. Is there anything the matter?"

"No. I'm going away now. I've done everything that's needed, and I don't think I've ever had so much pleasure in the company of a mortal, with the possible exception of your distinguished ancestress."

"Where are you going to?" she asked. "I don't really want you to go away. I've got very fond of you. Will you be back again?"

"No," replied the Indian, "I think I'll go to America. There isn't a great deal more that I can profitably spend my time on here. But I believe that there are certain experiments being conducted in the United States at the instigation of Dr. Einstein in a new kind of physics in which I am most interested. I can't say anything of it really, because it's rather secret at the present time. But I think I may be of some assistance. So I called to say good-by and to wish you well."

"It's all so wonderful," said Mrs. Pendlebury. "I still can't believe it. At one time it looked very bad indeed, when we were in the Tower. There's only one thing I don't understand."

"What is that?" asked Chief White Feather. His voice was little more than a whisper now.

"Well, why did Parson Pendlebury propose so suddenly that day, after he'd lost that paper—I wonder if he ever found it, poor man. He took me quite by surprise."

"That's a secret," said Chief White Feather. "I'm entitled to one secret and you mustn't inquire into it. Promise you won't?"

"I promise."

"Well, good-by now—and lots of luck." He bent swiftly and kissed her on the cheek. In a second he was gone completely, leaving Mrs. Pendlebury staring at the empty room.

There was a gentle knock at the door and the parson entered.

"My dear," he said, "we ought to be going if we're to catch our train."

"I'm ready now," she answered smiling.

As they walked down the stairs together the parson said, "It's the strangest thing, but I'm almost sure that just before I entered your room, a sort of shadow that looked in a fleeting glimpse like a Red Indian came out and I thought I heard him say, 'You're a very lucky man. Take good care of her.'"

She gave his hand a little squeeze.

"That was my guardian angel," she said, and they laughed together.

WHEN THE WAR WAS OVER, the villagers came back again as their forefathers had done before through the centuries. They brought a few German helmets and a few Japanese rifles and some big knives that said Blood and Honor on them in German and that would be useful for cutting mangolds up for cattle feed. The village hadn't changed much and they were glad of it because then they knew that they had really won.

The only changes were that the parson had a wife who came from London but whom everybody liked, and that the Fox and Hounds had been blown up and replaced by a new building.

Josiah Tanner had supervised the rebuilding himself and the new building was so very like the old that it was really hard to believe that it was new at all. There was only one real change and that was the signboard. It hung where the old one had hung but it now read:

THE FOX AND ROCKET
Beers and Stouts
Josiah Tanner, Prop.

When they got used to it, the villagers decided it was all right.

ANCIENT
HAUNTS

THE STONEGROUND
GHOST TALES
by E. G. Swain

TEDIOUS BRIEF TALES
OF GRANTA AND GRAMARYE
by Arthur Gray

ISBN 1-61646-005-9

COACHWHIP PUBLICATIONS

COACHWHIPBOOKS.COM

UNCANNY

UNCANNY STORIES AND
MORE UNCANNY STORIES
FROM *THE NOVEL MAGAZINE*

ISBN 1-61646-244-2

COACHWHIP PUBLICATIONS

ALSO AVAILABLE

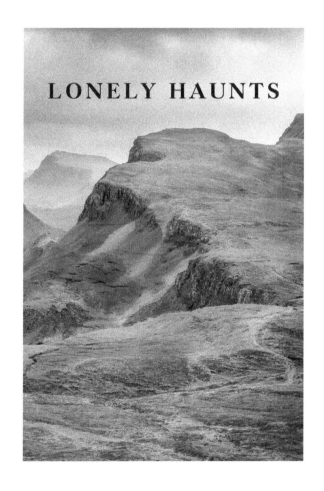

LONELY HAUNTS

ISBN 1-61646-249-3

CPSIA information can be obtained
at www.ICGtesting.com
Printed in the USA
BVHW031438041020
590262BV00003B/188